# VALENTINE'S POISON

Jim and Ginger Cozy Mysteries Book 5

Arthur Pearce

Copyright © 2025 Arthur Pearce

All rights reserved.

No part of this book may be reproduced, distributed, or transmitted in any form or by any means, including photocopying, recording, or other electronic or mechanical methods, without the prior written permission of the author, except in the case of brief quotations embodied in critical reviews and certain other noncommercial uses permitted by copyright law. For permission requests, please contact the author.

*"Valentine's Poison"* is a work of fiction. Names, characters, businesses, places, events and incidents either are products of the author's imagination or are used fictitiously. Any resemblance to actual persons, living or dead, events, or locales is entirely coincidental.

ISBN: 979-8-3058-7447-1

# Contents

| | |
|---|---|
| Chapter 1 | 1 |
| Chapter 2 | 15 |
| Chapter 3 | 29 |
| Chapter 4 | 39 |
| Chapter 5 | 53 |
| Chapter 6 | 65 |
| Chapter 7 | 79 |
| Chapter 8 | 91 |
| Chapter 9 | 105 |
| Chapter 10 | 117 |
| Chapter 11 | 129 |
| Chapter 12 | 145 |
| Chapter 13 | 157 |
| Chapter 14 | 167 |

| Chapter 15 | 179 |
| Chapter 16 | 191 |
| Chapter 17 | 203 |
| Chapter 18 | 217 |
| Chapter 19 | 231 |
| Chapter 20 | 243 |
| Jim and Ginger's Next Case | 255 |
| Bonus Content | 257 |
| Jim and Ginger's First Case | 259 |

# Chapter 1

The morning quiet shattered with the shrill ring of my phone, followed immediately by what sounded like a combination of whale songs and wind chimes. The sounds startled me awake from a pleasant dream involving a particularly well-organized library catalog system. I fumbled for the device, nearly knocking over my bedside lamp in the process.

"The phone is on your other side," Ginger observed from his perch on the windowsill, where he'd been watching the pre-dawn snowfall. "Your morning coordination continues to provide excellent entertainment.'"

I finally located the phone, managing to silence Emma's celestial wake-up call and answer just before it went to voicemail. "Hello?"

"Mr. Butterfield! Thank goodness you're awake!" Mrs. Henderson's voice carried its usual mix of urgency and theatrical distress. "I need you to come over right away. Something terrible has happened!"

I squinted at my bedside clock. 7:15 AM. Through the window, the street lights still glowed against the pre-dawn darkness, creating pools of warm light in the falling snow.

"Mrs. Henderson, is everything alright?"

"No! Everything is most certainly not alright. I've been robbed! Well, sort of robbed. In a very specific way. It's quite dramatic, really. You simply must come over and investigate!"

"Can this wait until after noon?" I asked, remembering Sophie's Valentine's Day celebration at the bakery. "We're supposed to-"

"Oh, this won't take long at all," she assured me with the confidence of someone who had never been brief about anything in her life. "But it's terribly important. Simply dreadful. And quite intriguing, if I do say so myself."

"Our neighbor's talent for making everything sound like a Victorian mystery novel remains impressive," Ginger commented, stretching languidly. "Though I notice her definition of 'emergency' tends to be rather flexible. Last week she called at midnight because she thought she saw a suspicious shadow in her garden. It turned out to be her own recycling bin."

I sighed, already knowing resistance was futile. Mrs. Henderson's determination was legendary in Oceanview Cove, surpassed only by her ability to turn the smallest incident into a town-wide drama. "Give us fifteen minutes."

"Wonderful! I'll put the kettle on. And Mr. Butterfield?" Her voice dropped to a conspiratorial whisper. "I have theories about who might be responsible. Very interesting theories indeed."

The line went dead before I could respond.

***

"Well," Ginger said, watching me struggle into my winter coat, "at least we know today won't be boring. Though I do hope whatever crisis has befallen our gossip-prone neighbor doesn't involve another missing garden gnome. The last one turned out to be simply buried under the snow, though not before Mrs. Henderson had developed an elaborate theory about gnome-napping rings operating along the Eastern seaboard."

The morning air bit sharply as we stepped outside. Fresh snow crunched under my boots as we made our way down the block.

Mrs. Henderson's Victorian house loomed against the pre-dawn sky, its gingerbread trim and multiple turrets creating a silhouette that wouldn't have looked out of place in a gothic novel. Unlike Mrs. Abernathy's meticulously maintained property down the street, Mrs. Henderson's showed signs of benign neglect. The paint was slightly faded, the garden contained what might have been artfully wild plants or simply weeds.

"I see our neighbor's dedication to spreading gossip continues to take precedence over home maintenance," Ginger observed as we approached the front door. "Though I must admit, the slightly haunted appearance does add a certain dramatic flair to her various crises."

Before I could knock, the door flew open. Mrs. Henderson stood there in a flower-print housecoat and fuzzy pink slippers with what appeared to be rabbit ears on them. Her silver hair was arranged in what appeared to be curlers, some of which seemed to be holding on more through optimism than actual grip. Her glasses sat slightly askew on her nose, magnifying her already prominent eyes, and she clutched a half-empty tea cup that sloshed dangerously with each gesture.

"Finally!" she exclaimed, ushering us inside with theatrical urgency. "I've been absolutely beside myself. Simply distraught. It's the most peculiar thing... Oh! Mind the pile of magazines by the door – I've been meaning to organize those. They contain some very interesting articles about mysterious happenings in coastal towns. Did you know there was a case in Maine where someone's entire collection of decorative lighthouses disappeared overnight?"

The house's interior carried the competing scents of furniture polish, aging wallpaper, and what might have been burnt toast. Unlike Mrs. Abernathy's precise organization, Mrs. Henderson's home showed signs of comfortable chaos. Stacks of magazines teetered on various surfaces, each pile looking like it might collapse at any moment. The walls were covered in framed photographs, their arrangement suggesting they'd been hung wherever space allowed rather than following any particular design. A collection of ceramic cats occupied most available shelf space, their painted eyes following our progress through the house with unsettling attention to detail.

A corgi with more enthusiasm than grace bounded down the hallway to greet us, its stubby tail wagging with enough force to threaten nearby decorative items. Several magazines lost their precarious balance as he passed, adding to the general disorder.

"Ah, I see Corky remembers our last encounter," Ginger said dryly, watching the dog's excited approach. "Though I notice his ability to corner effectively hasn't improved since our garden chase incident."

I smiled, remembering the incident Ginger was referring to – a complicated affair involving Mrs. Henderson's prized tuna sandwiches and what Ginger had deemed a "tactical sampling mission." Corky had pursued him through the garden with more determination than skill, eventually ending up tangled in a rosebush while Ginger watched from a safe perch, sandwich firmly secured. Mrs. Henderson had turned that into a three-week saga about potential sandwich-stealing rings targeting local gardens.

Mrs. Henderson led us into her parlor, where a tea service had been arranged on a cluttered coffee table. The teapot wore a hand-knitted cozy decorated with slightly lopsided hearts – presumably in honor of Valentine's Day. Beside it sat a plate of cookies that looked suspiciously like some of Mrs. Abernathy's recent experiments with exotic spices.

The room's focal point was a massive fireplace, its mantelpiece covered in what appeared to be Valentine's Day cards in various stages of aging. Each one seemed to have its own designated spot, though the overall arrangement had the same cheerful chaos as the rest of the house. A small space heater hummed nearby, suggesting the fireplace was more decorative than functional these days.

"It's absolutely dreadful," Mrs. Henderson declared, gesturing toward the mantel with her tea cup, creating a precarious arc of Earl Grey that somehow managed to miss everything in its path. "Simply devastating. My most precious Valentine's card – gone! Vanished! As if into thin air!"

"Our neighbor's talent for dramatic pauses rivals Emma's crystal readings," Ginger commented, settling onto a worn ottoman that offered a good view of both the mantel and Corky. The corgi had positioned himself near a bookshelf, his stubby tail still wagging with barely contained excitement as he nosed at something behind it.

The mantelpiece seemed to sag under the weight of decades' worth of Valentine's cards – some yellowed with age, others bright and recent. A conspicuous gap marked the center, like a missing tooth in an otherwise complete smile. Nearby, a collection of porcelain cupids aimed their arrows in various directions, creating what looked like a particularly disorganized firing squad.

"It was right here," Mrs. Henderson pointed, her voice quavering. "The most precious card in my collection.

From my Harold, fifty years ago this Valentine's Day." She dabbed at her eyes with a lace handkerchief that seemed to materialize from nowhere. "Simply irreplaceable. And the timing! Just when I'd been telling Mrs. Abernathy about its historical value..."

"When did you last see it?" I asked, accepting a cup of tea from Mrs. Henderson. The china was mismatched but clearly well-loved, each piece probably carrying its own story she'd be more than happy to share. My cup featured what appeared to be frolicking kittens wearing bowties.

"Yesterday evening, just before bed. After Mrs. Abernathy left – she came over for tea, you know. Though she was acting rather peculiar." Mrs. Henderson leaned forward, her voice dropping to what she probably thought was a whisper but could likely be heard next door. "Very interested in my Valentine collection. Kept asking questions about their value. And she's been experimenting with those new spices in her cookies – very suspicious if you ask me. Foreign spices!"

"Mrs. Abernathy? Really?" I couldn't quite keep the skepticism from my voice. The idea of our town's premier baker and cookie critic turning to Valentine card theft seemed about as likely as Miller voluntarily doing paperwork.

"Well, you never know," Mrs. Henderson sniffed, arranging cookies on a plate with more enthusiasm than precision. "Did you hear about her argument with Mr.

Whiskers last week? Over proper salmon preparation, of all things! If she's willing to fight with her own cat..."

"A gross misrepresentation of events," Ginger interjected, his tail twitching with indignation. "Mr. Whiskers simply expressed strong opinions about proper fish temperature. Though I must say, his culinary standards have become rather insufferable since Mrs. Abernathy started letting him sample her cooking. Last week he actually turned his nose up at perfectly good tuna because it wasn't 'properly seared.'"

"And then there were those children," Mrs. Henderson continued, warming to her theory as she poured more tea. Several drops escaped the cup's rim, creating a small archipelago of tea stains on the lace doily. "Three of them, came by asking for cookies while Mrs. Abernathy was here. Very suspicious timing, if you ask me. Though one did look remarkably like young Billy from the hardware store – you know, the one whose mother is supposedly seeing that mysterious fellow from the marina?"

She paused to sip her tea, clearly gathering momentum for more revelations. A curler chose that moment to give up its tenuous hold, dangling precariously near her left ear. "Speaking of suspicious relationships, have you heard about Mayor Thompson? His new secretary started just last month, and already there are rumors..." She wiggled her eyebrows meaningfully, causing the loose curler to swing like a pendulum. "Barbara says she's seen them having lunch together at Rose's café three times this week.

Three times! And apparently, they weren't even looking at menus..."

"About the card," I tried to redirect, recognizing the signs of an impending gossip avalanche. Through the window, I could see the sun finally clearing the horizon, painting the snow-covered street in shades of pink and gold. "What exactly did it look like?"

"Oh, it was beautiful," Mrs. Henderson sighed dreamily, temporarily distracted from her catalog of town scandals. "Hand-painted roses on the front, with real lace trim. Harold had it specially made by an artist in New York. Inside, he'd written the most wonderful poem..." She trailed off, lost in memory. "He was always so romantic, my Harold. Not like some people nowadays. Did you know the new dentist gave his wife a vacuum cleaner for Christmas? Can you imagine? Though speaking of vacuum cleaners, Mrs. Nelson told me the most fascinating story about her cousin's neighbor in Florida..."

Something caught my eye – a flash of movement near the bookshelf where Corky had been standing guard. The corgi's attention was fixed on something behind the heavy oak furniture, his excitement barely contained as he pawed at the baseboard.

"I see our short-legged friend has discovered something more interesting than his usual dust bunny collection," Ginger observed, watching Corky's increasingly excited behavior. "Though given the state of housekeeping behind that shelf, he might have found Jimmy Hoffa."

"Ginger?" I nodded toward the shelf. "Would you mind investigating?"

"Ah yes, what every cat dreams of – crawling behind dusty furniture while being observed by an overenthusiastic corgi," he muttered, but moved to inspect the area anyway. "I do hope you appreciate the sacrifices I make for our investigations. This dust is probably older than some of those Valentine's cards."

Mrs. Henderson was still expanding on her theories, which had somehow evolved to include international art thieves possibly targeting Valentine collections across the Eastern seaboard. Her hands gestured animatedly as she spoke, causing tiny tremors in her teacup that threatened to create new additions to the doily's growing collection of stains.

"And then there was that suspicious minivan parked down the street last week. Foreign license plates, I'm almost certain. Though I wasn't wearing my glasses at the time... but Barbara's sister's friend said she saw something similar in Rocky Point last month, right before the mysterious disappearance of a collection of antique love letters..."

"Found something," Ginger announced, his head poking out from behind the bookshelf. A cobweb decorated one ear like a delicate veil. "Mrs. Henderson's cleaning schedule behind here leaves much to be desired. I've seen cleaner dust bunnies in abandoned lighthouses. In fact, I believe I just discovered several generations of them holding a family reunion."

I moved to help him, carefully shifting the heavy shelf a few inches from the wall. A small avalanche of dust motes danced in the morning sunlight now streaming through the windows. There, partially hidden by what appeared to be several years' worth of accumulated history, lay a familiar-looking card. Its hand-painted roses and lace trim were unmistakable, even if slightly dusty.

"Mrs. Henderson?" I called, retrieving the card. "I believe we've solved your mystery."

She hurried over, adjusting her glasses and nearly tripping over Corky in the process. The loose curler swung wildly. "Oh! My precious Valentine! But how did it... why would someone hide it behind... unless..." Her eyes widened with fresh speculation. "Do you suppose the art thieves had accomplices? Maybe they were planning to retrieve it later! We should alert the authorities! I heard there's a special FBI division for Valentine-related crimes..."

"I don't think anyone hid it," I explained gently, brushing dust from the card's surface. "Look at these scratch marks on the corner. I suspect Corky might have batted it off the mantel during one of his more enthusiastic moments."

The corgi had the grace to look slightly ashamed, though his tail continued its perpetual motion. A dust bunny clung to his nose, making him sneeze.

"Corky!" Mrs. Henderson gasped, though her tone carried more relief than anger. "You naughty boy! I suppose this means Mrs. Abernathy isn't secretly building a Valentine card empire..." She brightened suddenly. "But speaking of Mrs. Abernathy, did you hear about her new cookie recipe? Those exotic spices I mentioned? Well, apparently, she's been seen making late-night visits to that mysterious spice shop in the city. The one owned by that woman who might have been in the circus. Or was it the foreign legion? Barbara wasn't quite clear on that part..."

"Actually," I interrupted, checking my watch, "we really should be going. Sophie's Valentine's Day celebration starts soon, and-"

"Oh, but you simply must see the rest of my collection first!" Mrs. Henderson was already moving toward a large cabinet, narrowly avoiding another pile of magazines. "I have cards from every decade since the 1920s! This one here belonged to my great-aunt Mildred – such a scandal about her and the lighthouse keeper. Did you know they used to signal each other with lanterns? Very romantic, though the shipping companies weren't too pleased about it. Three boats nearly ran aground before anyone realized what was happening..."

"Our neighbor's ability to connect any topic to a historical scandal remains unmatched," Ginger observed, watching Mrs. Henderson rifle through her collection. "But the lighthouse keeper story explains some of last summer's navigation issues. Apparently, poor sense of direction runs in the family."

"Perhaps another time," I suggested firmly, edging toward the door. "We wouldn't want to be late for Sophie's event."

"Oh, yes, Sophie's celebration," Mrs. Henderson nodded knowingly, finally abandoning her cabinet expedition. "Though have you heard about her secret midnight baking sessions? Martha swears she saw mysterious lights in the bakery at 3 AM last week, and the most extraordinary smells... Like nothing we've had in town before. And just yesterday, someone spotted her having a very intense conversation with a man in a fancy suit – apparently a French pastry critic traveling incognito! Though between you and me," she lowered her voice conspiratorially, "I heard he might actually be her long-lost culinary school sweetheart, come to whisk her away to Paris..."

We managed to make our escape, though Mrs. Henderson's voice followed us onto the porch: "Oh! And before you go – did you hear about what happened at Rose's café last night? Someone saw her testing secret recipes after hours, and there were the most peculiar colored lights in the kitchen windows! And sounds that could only be described as..."

The door closed behind us, muffling whatever culinary intrigue she'd been about to share. The morning had fully arrived now, transforming the street into a pristine white landscape. The sun sparkled off the fresh snow, creating tiny rainbows that would have delighted Emma's mystical sensibilities.

"Well," Ginger said as we made our way carefully down the slippery porch steps, "that was certainly an interesting start to Valentine's Day. Our neighbor's talent for turning a simple missing card into an international conspiracy remains undiminished. Next time, we should sell tickets – 'Mrs. Henderson's Morning Mysteries: Now featuring suspicious spice merchants and lighthouse romance scandals.'"

"At least it wasn't another garden gnome situation," I replied, remembering the three-hour search last month that ended when a particularly energetic game of fetch between Corky and the neighbor's retriever revealed an entire collection of ceramic figures buried under a snowdrift. Mrs. Henderson had been convinced they'd organized their own migration.

"Indeed," Ginger agreed, delicately picking his way through the snow. "Though I must say, Corky's involvement adds a certain poetic justice to the situation. A corgi named Corky causing chaos – it's like a children's book gone slightly wrong."

We turned toward Sophie's bakery, where warm lights already glowed in the windows despite the early hour. The scent of fresh bread and Valentine's treats drifted on the morning air, promising a celebration that would hopefully involve fewer missing cards and international conspiracies.

# Chapter 2

The morning sun painted Sophie's bakery in shades of pink and gold as we approached, the windows frosted with delicate heart patterns that seemed too precise to be natural. The scent of fresh pastries and warm bread wrapped around us like a welcome embrace, carrying hints of vanilla, chocolate, and something more exotic that I couldn't quite identify.

Inside, the transformation was complete. Pink and red hearts cascaded from the ceiling in artful arrangements, while delicate paper flowers bloomed along the walls. Soft lighting caught the metallic sheen of Valentine's decorations, creating a warm glow that somehow managed to be festive without crossing into gaudy. Small red and white lanterns had been strung across the ceiling, casting a gentle, romantic light.

The bakery buzzed with pre-celebration energy, townspeople already gathering despite the early hour. The usual display cases had been rearranged to create a more open space, with small tables draped in white linens dotting the floor. Each table bore a centerpiece of fresh flowers and what appeared to be hand-crafted paper hearts, probably Sophie's work. The air was rich with the mingled aromas of fresh coffee, warm pastries, and the particular excitement that seems to accompany any special occasion in a small town.

Brenda Evans looked up from where she was adjusting a particularly elaborate heart display, her movements precise despite her obvious excitement. She'd worked at the bakery for nearly two weeks now, ever since Sophie had hired her as a temporary replacement for Alice. Today she wore a crisp white apron over practical clothes, her dark hair pulled back in a neat bun that suggested efficiency rather than style. A small heart-shaped pin glinted on her collar, catching the morning light.

"Mr. Butterfield! And Ginger too!" She smiled warmly, though I noticed her fingers continued their automatic straightening of the display. "I was worried Mrs. Henderson might keep you all morning with her theories about mysterious Valentine card thieves. She called here twice already to warn us about suspicious minivans in the area."

"News travels fast," I observed, watching her make minute adjustments to an already perfect arrangement. The hearts seemed to dance slightly in the warm air from the ovens, creating shifting patterns on the walls.

"Small towns," she shrugged, finally satisfied with the heart's position. "Though I hear she's expanded the theory to include international art dealers and something about a suspicious minivan with foreign license plates? And apparently there's a connection to missing garden gnomes from last month?"

"Our temporary baker seems remarkably well-informed about local gossip," Ginger commented, his tail swishing thoughtfully. "Though I notice her attention to detail with those decorations suggests either artistic dedication or mild obsession. Perhaps we should introduce her to Emma – they could compare notes on proper alignment of decorative elements."

Before I could respond, a booming voice carried across the bakery: "Butterfield! Finally get to meet the famous detective in person!"

Mayor Thompson approached, already sampling what appeared to be some kind of elaborately frosted pastry. Powdered sugar dusted his expensive suit, suggesting this wasn't his first treat of the morning. A small trail of crumbs marked his path across the bakery floor like breadcrumbs in a fairy tale. He cut an imposing figure – tall, broad-shouldered, with the kind of carefully maintained silver hair that spoke of regular visits to an upscale barber. His suit probably cost more than most townsfolk made in a month, though he'd paired it with a garish Valentine's themed tie that featured what appeared to be cupids playing jazz instruments.

"Heard all about your cases," he continued, extending his free hand while somehow managing to maintain his grip on a half-eaten pastry. A signet ring caught the light as we shook hands, the town seal glinting importantly.

"Quite impressive work! That Christmas tree business especially – saved us from quite a bit of trouble, let me tell you. Though the insurance company still sends me concerned letters about rigged Christmas trees."

He brushed some powdered sugar from his lapel, creating a small snowfall on his already well-dusted shoes. "You know, I could probably arrange an official position with the police department. God knows Miller could use the help. Man spends more time organizing his donut collection than actual evidence. Just last week he filed a noise complaint under 'P' for 'Particularly Loud' – took us three days to find it."

"And here I thought the Christmas tree incident would have inspired him to improve his filing system," I said, remembering Miller's confusion over where to categorize "mechanical holiday decorations with homicidal tendencies."

"Improve? Ha!" The mayor laughed, sending more powdered sugar flying. "He's added a new category called 'Festive Mayhem.' Claims it helps him prepare for holiday-related crimes."

I remembered Mrs. Henderson's gossip about the mayor and his new secretary. "Quite a crowd this morning," I observed casually. "Though I notice your secretary couldn't make it?"

The mayor's face reddened faster than one of Sophie's thermometers during a hot cross bun emergency. He suddenly became very interested in his half-eaten pastry, examining it like it might contain the secrets of the universe. "Ah, well, busy time at the office, you know. Lots of... paperwork. Important civic documents. Can't file themselves, ha ha!" His laugh carried a slight edge of panic. "Speaking of which, these treats are extraordinary! Brenda here was kind enough to let me sample a few early." He winked at Brenda, who smiled back with practiced charm while adjusting yet another heart display.

"The benefits of being mayor," Brenda said cheerfully, though I noticed she carefully moved another tray of pastries just out of his reach. "Though perhaps we should save some for the other guests? Sophie and I spent hours on these special Valentine's designs."

"Of course, of course," the mayor agreed, even as his eyes tracked the movement of the tray. "Though as mayor, it's my civic duty to ensure the quality of local establishments. Very important responsibility, quality control."

Suddenly, the mayor's expression shifted. His hand moved to his stomach, which emitted an audible growl that somehow managed to sound both urgent and mayoral. "Ah, Brenda? The facilities...?"

"Through the kitchen door, first door on the left," she replied smoothly, already moving to guide him. "Let me show you. Mind the new delivery of flour – we had to stack it in the hallway."

They disappeared toward the back, the mayor moving with rather more urgency than dignity. His usual confident stride had been replaced by something closer to a controlled power walk. Several townspeople poorly concealed their amusement behind hands and napkins, while others exchanged knowing looks.

"I see the mayor's sweet tooth remains undefeated," Chuck chuckled from his corner table, stirring his coffee with deliberate slowness. "Though I suspect his appetite might have finally met its match."

"Now Chuck," Mrs. Nelson scolded from the next table, though her eyes twinkled with amusement. "We shouldn't laugh at others' misfortunes." She paused, then added with a small smile, "At least not until they're out of earshot."

"Speaking of hearing things," old Mrs. Davis piped up, adjusting her shawl, "did anyone else notice how quickly he changed the subject when his secretary was mentioned? Very interesting, wouldn't you say?"

"Almost as interesting as those three lunch meetings at Rose's café," Chuck agreed, reaching for another cookie.

"The mayor's dining habits seem to inspire quite the political discourse," Ginger observed dryly. "Though I notice our local analysts' dedication to detailed observation rivals Mrs. Henderson's. Perhaps we should suggest they start an investigation agency of their own."

Mrs. Abernathy approached our small group, Mr. Whiskers following with his usual regal air. "The mayor certainly seemed eager to sample those pastries," she said, adjusting her apron with precise movements. "But his technique leaves much to be desired. Three bites for a proper éclair evaluation, taken from different angles – that's the proper way. Not that anyone asks my professional opinion anymore." She sniffed disapprovingly.

"Except every Tuesday at the cookie critique club," Chuck reminded her with a grin. "Or have you forgotten last week's great shortbread debate?"

"That was different," Mrs. Abernathy insisted. "Those were technical discussions about proper butter distribution. Very scientific. Speaking of which..." She turned toward the kitchen, raising her voice slightly. "Sophie dear, I noticed the lamination on those croissants seems a bit uneven on the left side. We should discuss proper folding technique later."

Emma's table drew my attention – she'd transformed her corner of the bakery into something between a fortune-telling parlor and a crystal showroom. A massive rose quartz specimen dominated the center, surrounded by smaller crystals arranged in what I assumed was some cosmically significant pattern. Her outfit today outdid even her usual mystical attire – a dress covered in actual twinkling lights arranged in real constellations, complete with a small meteor shower cascading down one sleeve.

"Jim! Ginger!" She brightened as we approached, her numerous bangles creating their usual symphony. Several crystals on her table actually vibrated in response to her enthusiastic greeting. "The stars suggested you'd be delayed by Mrs. Henderson's crisis. But they were a bit vague about whether it involved missing valentines or mysterious garden gnomes. Venus is in a particularly tricky position this morning."

"Just valentines this time," I assured her, watching as she adjusted a particularly large crystal that seemed to be trying to escape its cosmic alignment. "No gnome emergency today. I notice Shawn and Robert aren't here yet?"

Emma's hands danced over her crystals, each movement precise despite the apparent chaos of her arrangement. "Robert's still out at sea," she replied, pausing to consult what appeared to be a star chart covered in coffee stains and cookie crumbs. "Something about checking his nets before the storm that's coming in a few days. My celestial weather predictions have been quite accurate lately – I warned him about the low pressure system three days ago. Though he claimed it was the weather service that tipped him off." She sniffed disapprovingly at such mundane methods of forecasting.

"And Shawn's accepting a delivery at the bar – apparently there's a new craft brewery he's trying. But the crystals suggest both will join us later." She leaned forward, lowering her voice conspiratorially. "Unless Mercury's retrograde position interferes with their timing. It's been causing all sorts of scheduling chaos. Did you know it made Mrs. Abernathy's cat show up ten minutes early for his morning cookie tasting? The cosmic balance is clearly disturbed."

A familiar orange shape caught my eye – Mr. Whiskers had claimed his usual position of superiority on the highest windowsill, his massive bulk somehow managing to look both regal and slightly smug. His Persian fur had been groomed to maximum effect, creating an impressive mane that caught the morning light like a feline crown. His golden eyes fixed on Ginger with his usual mix of disdain and territorial challenge.

"I see his imperial majesty continues to claim the premium observation posts," Ginger commented, settling into a dignified sitting position. "Though I notice his grooming seems somewhat hurried today. That left ear tuft is positively rebellious. Perhaps Mrs. Abernathy's morning cookie critiques ran longer than usual?"

As if summoned by Ginger's words, the kitchen doors swung open with theatrical timing. Sophie emerged first, carrying a tray laden with what appeared to be heart-shaped pastries dusted with iridescent sugar that caught the light like tiny prisms. Steam rose from them in delicate spirals, carrying the mingled aromas of butter, vanilla, and something more exotic that made several waiting customers lean forward unconsciously.

Mrs. Abernathy followed with her own tray of elaborately decorated cookies, each one looking like a miniature work of art. She'd clearly been up since dawn working on them – I recognized her particular style in the precise lines of royal icing and the mathematically perfect distribution of sprinkles. Her usual practical attire had been enhanced with a heart-shaped pin that looked suspiciously like one of Emma's cosmic crafting projects.

Brenda brought up the rear, somehow managing three trays with impressive dexterity. Her poise suggested years of waiting tables or perhaps juggling – the trays barely trembled as she navigated around Emma's crystal-laden table and Mrs. Nelson's strategically extended cane.

"Watch your step there, dear," Mrs. Davis called out as Brenda expertly sidestepped a stray crystal that had rolled from Emma's table. "I notice you handle those trays like a professional."

"Years of practice," Brenda smiled, setting down her burdens with careful precision. "Though never with pastries quite this beautiful. Sophie's been teaching me her techniques – when she's not creating new masterpieces, that is."

The treats were arranged on tables with the kind of precision that suggested hours of planning. Each table received its own unique selection, the colors and patterns creating an edible rainbow across the bakery. Tiny heart-shaped macarons nestled next to chocolate truffles that gleamed like polished stones. Delicate pastries filled with fresh cream and berries sat proudly on silver stands, while cookies decorated with intricate Valentine messages formed elegant towers.

"The detail work on these is extraordinary," Mrs. Abernathy admitted, examining a particularly elaborate chocolate creation. "Though the ganache could perhaps use a touch more cream. For optimal shine, you understand."

Then Sophie reached under the counter and produced another tray, this one holding what appeared to be her pièce de résistance – delicate pastries that seemed to shimmer in the morning light. Each one had been crafted to look like a miniature Valentine, complete with tiny edible "stamps" and "postmarks" made from colored chocolate. The detail was extraordinary – you could almost read the tiny love messages piped onto each one.

"Now those," Mrs. Abernathy declared, her usual critical tone softening slightly, "are absolutely perfect."

Sophie's eyes narrowed slightly as she surveyed the display, noting the gaps where certain treats should have been. The missing pastries left small empty spaces in the otherwise perfect arrangement, like missing teeth in a smile. Her gaze shifted to Brenda, who smiled apologetically while adjusting a heart-shaped cream puff that had attempted to escape its designated spot.

"The mayor was very persuasive," Brenda explained, rescuing another pastry that seemed determined to roll off the edge of its tray. "He said something about needing to properly evaluate the town's culinary achievements. For official purposes, of course."

"Speaking of our esteemed leader," Chuck called out from his corner table, where he'd been strategically positioned near the chocolate section, "is he still... indisposed?"

Brenda's lips twitched as she straightened yet another wayward treat. "Let's just say he's learning about portion control the hard way. Though I did warn him that the triple chocolate mousse bombs were meant to be shared."

A ripple of poorly suppressed laughter moved through the growing crowd. Mrs. Abernathy smiled as she adjusted an already perfect display of heart-shaped macarons, her eyes twinkling with amusement. Mr. Whiskers, still maintaining his regal perch on the windowsill, managed to look both amused and disapproving at such undignified behavior.

The proper celebration began as more townspeople filtered in, drawn by the warmth and promise of Sophie's creations. The usual morning quiet of the bakery gave way to the happy buzz of conversation and occasional exclamations of delight as people discovered particularly impressive treats. Emma's corner maintained a steady stream of visitors, each leaving with predictions that somehow managed to involve both romance and proper pastry appreciation.

"The stars suggest you'll meet someone special over coffee and croissants," she told Mrs. Nelson, her crystals creating tiny rainbows as she moved them in apparently significant patterns. "Though Venus warns against sampling the chocolate eclairs before the third date. And do be careful with the raspberry tarts – Mars is in a particularly passionate position today."

Sophie had even prepared special treats for the bakery's feline visitors. A small plate near the window held delicacies that looked more elegant than most human desserts I'd seen. Tiny fish-shaped pastries decorated with edible scales sat beside what appeared to be salmon mousse piped into delicate rosettes.

"I must say," Ginger observed from his position near the plate, "Sophie has outdone herself with the feline refreshments. Though I notice Mr. Whiskers seems unusually interested in that particular platter of salmon-based delicacies. His territorial ambitions apparently extend to cuisine as well as windowsills. And his approach to that mousse suggests his usual dignified demeanor might not survive contact with premium seafood."

I had to agree – all the treats were extraordinary. A delicate passionfruit mousse literally melted on my tongue, while a dark chocolate creation carried hints of what might have been exotic spices. The traditional cookies had been elevated to art forms, each one decorated with the kind of precision that spoke of hours of careful work.

The morning light streamed through the windows, catching the falling sugar like diamond dust. The bakery had transformed into something magical – not just from the decorations and treats, but from the genuine warmth and joy that filled the space. Even Mr. Whiskers had abandoned his usual aloof dignity enough to accept a specially crafted treat from Mrs. Abernathy's hand, though he maintained his superior expression while doing so.

Through the kitchen door, I caught glimpses of Sophie and Brenda working in perfect sync, bringing out fresh trays to replace the rapidly diminishing displays. Their movements had the practiced efficiency of dancers who knew their routine by heart. Brenda seemed to anticipate Sophie's needs before they arose, already reaching for the next tray or adjusting a display that needed refreshing.

Suddenly, a loud growl echoed across the bakery. Chuck's face reddened as he clutched his stomach. "Oh dear," he muttered, pushing himself up from his chair with surprising speed. He hurried toward the kitchen, disappearing through the doors. Barely a minute later, he emerged looking distinctly uncomfortable.

"That blasted toilet's still occupied!" he announced to no one in particular, already heading for the exit. "Mayor Thompson's been in there for half an hour!" Without another word, he hustled out of the bakery at a pace that belied his age, leaving behind a wave of poorly suppressed giggles.

I found myself chuckling at the scene, but my amusement was short-lived.

Ginger's voice, suddenly uncertain, caught my attention. "Jim?" The usual sarcasm was gone, replaced by something that made my heart skip. "I don't feel quite..."

I turned just in time to see my feline partner sway slightly, his usual grace deserting him. His steps faltered as he tried to move away from the treat plate. The bakery's cheerful atmosphere seemed to dim as worry crept in.

Something was wrong.

# Chapter 3

I couldn't process Ginger's sudden weakness, my mind refusing to accept the sight of my usually composed partner swaying unsteadily. His eyes, normally sharp with sarcasm, had dulled to a glassy sheen. I reached for him just as his legs gave out, gathering him carefully in my arms. His familiar weight felt wrong somehow – too limp, too quiet.

"Just resting my eyes," he muttered, but his usual wit lacked its edge. "Though I must say, your hands are shaking more than Emma's crystal collection during an earthquake."

Before I could respond, chaos erupted across the bakery. Mrs. Nelson clutched her stomach, her face turning an alarming shade of pale. She stumbled toward the door, nearly colliding with Chuck's abandoned chair. Her usually perfect hat tilted at a precarious angle as she made her hasty exit.

Behind her, Emma swayed in her seat, her constellation dress twinkling erratically as she slumped forward onto her crystal-laden table. Several stones rolled across the floor, their cosmic alignment thoroughly disrupted. A particularly large rose quartz spun away like a runaway planet, narrowly missing Mrs. Davis's foot.

"The celestial energies..." Emma managed weakly before her eyes rolled back. She collapsed onto her star charts, scattering coffee-stained predictions across the floor.

Mrs. Abernathy's hand flew to her mouth, her usual composed demeanor cracking as she watched the chaos unfold. Even Mr. Whiskers abandoned his regal perch, his expression turning from dignified to desperate as he raced toward the door with uncharacteristic urgency.

The bakery's warm atmosphere dissolved into pandemonium. People who'd been happily sampling treats moments ago now clutched their stomachs or grabbed for support. Some rushed for the exits while others simply collapsed where they stood. The air filled with groans and the sound of chairs scraping against the floor as people either fled or fell.

One of the fishermen made another attempt at the bathroom door, pounding desperately. "Thompson! For heaven's sake, man, there are other people in crisis here!"

A muffled groan from inside suggested the mayor was in no condition to accommodate other visitors. The door remained firmly locked.

A sharp cramp hit my own stomach with the subtlety of a sledgehammer. The pain doubled me over, nearly causing me to drop Ginger. Cold sweat broke out on my forehead as I did some rapid calculations. The bakery's only bathroom was still occupied by the mayor's ongoing gastrointestinal crisis. My house was too far – I'd never make it. That left only one option: my office, barely five minutes away.

I carefully placed Ginger on the table, making sure he was stable. "Stay here," I managed through clenched teeth. "I'll be back as soon as I can."

"Yes, because I had such elaborate plans for the next few minutes," he mumbled, his usual sarcasm weakened but still present. "Perhaps a quick marathon or some light parkour..."

Another cramp hit, this one worse than the first. I barely registered Sophie's concerned voice somewhere behind me as I burst through the bakery door into the winter morning. The cold air hit like a slap, but I barely noticed as I broke into what could generously be called a run.

I cursed my winter-induced fitness lapse as I stumbled through the snow. The morning joggers who usually passed my window had the right idea – though I doubted any of them had anticipated this particular motivation for cardio training. My breath came in ragged gasps, creating small clouds that mockingly marked my slow progress.

A patch of ice nearly ended my desperate journey right there, sending me pinwheeling past a startled Mrs. Henderson who was hurrying down the sidewalk, bundled in her winter coat and woolen scarf, several curlers still clinging valiantly to her hair beneath her hat.

"Mr. Butterfield!" she called out. "Did you see that suspicious minivan just- oh my! Are you quite alright? You look rather... urgent. Though speaking of urgent matters, did you know there's been a series of mysterious stomach ailments reported in coastal towns recently? Barbara's cousin's neighbor in Maine said-"

I lurched past without responding, unable to spare breath for what would undoubtedly become a lengthy discourse on gastrointestinal conspiracies spanning the Eastern seaboard.

"The minivan had foreign license plates!" she called after me. "And the driver was wearing a very suspicious hat!"

Three minutes felt like three hours. Each step brought a new appreciation for just how far five blocks could feel. The winter crowds seemed determined to block my path – I dodged around a group of tourists admiring the town hall's icicles, narrowly avoided a delivery truck backing out of the Harbor View café, and nearly collided with a dog walker juggling three leashes and a coffee cup.

"Watch it!" the walker called out as her poodle mixture expressed its opinion of my erratic movement with a series of high-pitched barks. "Some of us are trying to- sir? Are you okay? You look a bit..."

I waved off her concern without breaking stride, though "stride" was perhaps too generous a term for my current locomotion. More like "controlled stumbling with occasional bursts of panic."

The universe seemed determined to test my endurance. A group of seagulls had chosen this exact moment to hold what appeared to be an emergency conference in my path, scattering with indignant squawks as I barreled through their meeting. Their loud protests followed me down the street, probably adding another chapter to Mrs. Henderson's conspiracy theories.

"Did you see that suspicious character running through town?" I could almost hear her telling Barbara later. "Acting very peculiar, disrupting perfectly innocent seagull gatherings. And on Valentine's Day, no less!"

My office door had never looked so beautiful. I fumbled with the keys, my hands shaking from both cold and urgency. The lock fought back with the peculiar stubbornness of inanimate objects that sense desperation. After what felt like several geological ages but was probably only seconds, the door finally surrendered.

I barely made it.

Time lost all meaning in a blur of discomfort that I won't describe in detail. Let's just say I gained a new appreciation for the mayor's extended bathroom occupation at the bakery. I also made several solemn promises to whatever cosmic forces might be listening about resuming my morning exercise routine, though I suspected Emma would say the planets were too misaligned for such bargaining.

"Next time," I muttered to myself, "I'm installing one of those fancy Japanese toilets with all the features. And maybe a small library. And an emergency phone line."

When I finally emerged, weak but somewhat stabilized, my office clock showed nearly an hour had passed since I'd left the bakery. Guilt and worry about Ginger hit immediately – I needed to get back. The walk that had seemed endless earlier now felt torturously slow as I forced myself to move carefully, my stomach still uncertain about this whole concept of movement.

Mrs. Henderson had expanded her surveillance operation, now accompanied by several neighbors who seemed equally invested in monitoring suspicious activities. Their whispered conversations carried across the street as I passed.

"And then he ran past, looking absolutely green! Just like those mysterious figures Barbara's sister saw in Newport last month. Though they were wearing matching h ats..."

\*\*\*

The scene that greeted me at the bakery stopped me cold. Two ambulances parked haphazardly near the entrance, their emergency lights painting the snow in alternating red and white. Police cars had joined them, their presence suggesting this had escalated well beyond a simple case of collective indigestion. A small crowd of onlookers had gathered at a safe distance, their murmured conversations carrying traces of both concern and the particular excitement that accompanies any dramatic event in a small town.

Officer Martinez stood near the door, taking notes as Mrs. Abernathy spoke. Her usual perfect posture had wilted slightly, though she maintained her dignity even in obvious discomfort. Mr. Whiskers perched in her arms, his magnificent fur distinctly ruffled, suggesting he'd spent the last hour much as I had.

"And then they just started dropping," Mrs. Abernathy was saying, absently stroking Mr. Whiskers's fur. "Like a soufflé in an earthquake."

Inside, the bakery's festive atmosphere had transformed into something from a disaster movie. Fallen decorations littered the floor, creating a sad confetti of crushed paper hearts. Several chairs lay overturned, marking where people had either collapsed or fled. Emma's crystal display had scattered across the floor, the stones catching the morning light like tears. A particularly large amethyst had somehow ended up in a half-eaten éclair, creating what Emma would probably call a "cosmic-culinary convergence."

Dr. Chen knelt beside a still form near the counter, a white sheet obscuring most details. My heart clenched until I noticed the figure was too large to be Ginger. The doctor's movements were precise and professional as she made notes, though her expression carried the weight of someone delivering bad news.

My eyes scanned the room frantically, searching for an orange shape that wasn't there. The table where I'd left Ginger stood empty except for fallen decorations and abandoned treats. Panic rose in my throat.

"Mr. Butterfield!" Dr. Chen's voice cut through my growing fear. She stood, tucking her notebook into a pocket of her practical coat. "I was wondering when you'd be back. Feeling better?"

"Marginally," I managed. "Ginger?"

"He's at the hospital," she assured me quickly. "Shawn came by earlier – said he was heading to the Salty Breeze to accept a delivery when he saw the commotion. He took both Ginger and Emma to the emergency room. Found them both unconscious."

Relief made my knees weak. "Will they be okay?"

"The symptoms suggest yes." She nodded toward the sheet-covered form. "Unlike Mr. Edison here. The hospital reports several cases of fainting, like Ginger and Emma, plus a significant number of... digestive issues." A slight smile touched her lips. "The mayor is still occupying the bakery's facilities, by the way. His wife called twice already."

"What happened?" I asked, watching as Sophie spoke with two officers near the kitchen. Her usual cheerful demeanor had vanished, replaced by something closer to shock. Beside her, Brenda worked methodically to clean up fallen decorations, her movements automatic, as if keeping her hands busy helped maintain composure. Officer Martinez had moved his interview with Mrs. Abernathy inside, where she cradled a distinctly ruffled Mr. Whiskers.

"Mass poisoning, from initial evidence." Dr. Chen's voice dropped lower. "Two distinct substances, as far as we can tell. One appears to be a powerful laxative – as many of the Valentine's Day celebration guests has unfortunately discovered." She raised an eyebrow knowingly. "The other is more concerning. It causes unconsciousness in about ten to fifteen minutes after consumption, and in Mr. Edison's case..." She gestured toward the covered form.

"He was eighty-nine," she continued, her professional tone softening slightly. "Had a history of heart problems. The combination of these substances, plus the shock to his system... it was too much. He never had a chance."

I remembered Mr. Edison from Shawn's stories – the former principal of that abandoned school from our Christmas case. After retiring, he'd tried his hand at business ventures and local investments, though success had proved elusive. Just last week, Shawn mentioned seeing him at the bar, still talking about his latest investment ideas despite his age.

My gaze drifted back to Sophie. Her hands twisted her apron as she spoke with the officers, her eyes bright with unshed tears. Could she have followed in her sister's footsteps? The thought seemed impossible, yet Maggie had seemed equally unlikely as a murderer until she wasn't.

"I know what you're thinking," Dr. Chen said quietly. "But let's wait for the toxicology reports before jumping to conclusions. This feels... different from Maggie's methods. Less calculated, more chaotic." She straightened her practical coat. "Though I wouldn't count on Miller seeing those nuances. He'll want a simple solution – probably blame it on food storage temperatures or something equally convenient."

She checked her watch. "I should get Mr. Edison's body to the morgue. Time is critical with poisoning cases." Her expression softened slightly. "Go see Ginger. The investigation can wait – he needs you more right now."

I glanced again at Sophie, still talking with the officers. Her shoulders had slumped, exhaustion and worry evident in every line of her body. Part of me wanted to stay, to start unraveling this mystery immediately. But Dr. Chen was right – some things were more important than investigation.

The investigation could wait.

# Chapter 4

The Oceanview Cove Hospital dominated the morning skyline, its weathered brick walls a testament to decades of small-town medical care. Windows stretched across all four stories, reflecting the weak winter sun. Though I'd passed by hundreds of times on my way to the harbor, this was my first time actually entering. Through the emergency department's sliding doors, I could hear raised voices and the particular chaos that accompanies any small-town crisis.

The waiting room churned with a mix of Valentine's Day celebration victims and the usual emergency department regulars. Several people I recognized from the bakery sat holding their stomachs, looking distinctly green. Chuck had claimed a corner chair, his usual dignified posture abandoned in favor of what looked like a deeply uncomfortable slouch. Near him, Mrs. Davis clutched her signature shawl, her face pale beneath her carefully applied makeup. Even the usually boisterous fishermen who'd been at the celebration sat quietly, their robust frames diminished by discomfort.

The air carried the competing scents of antiseptic and anxiety, underscored by the steady beep of monitors and squeak of rubber-soled shoes on linoleum. A harried-looking nurse dealt with a line of people at the intake desk, her efficiency suggesting long practice with emergency department triage. Her name tag read "Linda," and she somehow managed to type, answer phones, and direct traffic all while maintaining an air of calm control. The ancient TV mounted in one corner played a soap opera that no one seemed to be watching, its drama somehow less interesting than the real-life version unfolding around us.

A young mother tried to comfort her crying child while simultaneously filling out paperwork. The boy had apparently sampled several of Sophie's special Valentine's treats, judging by the chocolate stains on his shirt and the way he clutched his stomach. His sister sat beside them, looking queasy but determined not to admit it.

"Jim!"

I turned to find Shawn waving from near a cluster of worn chairs that had probably witnessed decades of similar dramas. His bartender's apron bore traces of flour from the bakery chaos, and his expression carried equal parts relief and concern as he waved me over.

"Thank God," he said as I approached. "Was starting to worry about you too. Though from what Chuck said about 'that bastard Thompson,' I had a pretty good idea where you'd disappeared to."

I settled into a chair whose upholstery had seen better days. A spring dug into my back, suggesting it had opinions about proper posture. "What happened? How did you find them?"

Shawn ran a hand through his hair, leaving it standing at odd angles. He'd clearly been through an ordeal himself. "Was on my way to the bar – new craft brewery delivery, you know how it is. That Imperial Stout I've been trying to get for months finally came in." He shook his head, as if surprised by how normal that detail seemed now. "I was still a block away when I saw the commotion. People stumbling out of Sophie's place holding their stomachs. Then Chuck nearly knocked me over, cursing about Thompson monopolizing the bathroom and 'mayors who think they own everything, including other people's toilets.'"

A nurse hurried past with an armful of supplies, her shoes squeaking against the well-worn linoleum. The intake desk phone rang again, adding to the symphony of hospital sounds.

"Went inside to check," Shawn continued, lowering his voice. "Found total chaos. Display cases knocked over, treats scattered everywhere. Emma was out cold by her crystals, looked like she'd face-planted right into her star charts. Her dress was still doing that twinkling thing – you know how she loves those light-up constellations. And Ginger..." He shook his head, his expression darkening.

"Never seen him so still. Not a whisker twitching. Scared me, if I'm being honest."

"So you brought them here?"

"Straight away. Called an ambulance first, but with all the chaos, figured it'd be faster to bring them myself. Emma's light enough to carry, and Ginger..." A small smile touched his face. "Let's just say he'd be mortified to know I carried him wrapped in my bar apron. Though it was clean," he added quickly. "Fresh from the laundry this morning."

"The doctors agreed to treat Ginger?" I shifted in my chair, trying to avoid the rebellious spring.

"Didn't even question it." Shawn's smile widened slightly. "Nurse recognized him from that Christmas tree case – she was there that New Year's Eve at the square with her kids. Said she saw Ginger find that mechanism in time, before the tree could fall. They're treating him like any other patient. Even put him in with Emma – something about 'keeping the cosmic energy aligned.' Think they've been reading too many of Emma's horoscopes in the town paper."

Heavy footsteps approached – Robert appeared, still wearing his fishing gear, salt water dripping from his coat to form small puddles on the linoleum. His face showed the particular worry of someone who'd rushed from the harbor without bothering to change. The scent of fish and sea air followed him, creating an odd contrast with the hospital's antiseptic atmosphere.

"Just heard," Robert said, dropping into a nearby chair. The plastic creaked ominously under his bulk, another piece of furniture protesting its existence. "Damn cell service out on the water – missed three calls before I got the message. How are they?"

An orderly wheeled past with an empty gurney, its wheels adding another layer to the hospital's constant background noise. Through the waiting room windows, I could see more people arriving, their faces showing various stages of Valentine's Day distress.

"Doctors say they should recover," Shawn replied, absently brushing flour dust from his sleeve. "Just need time to rest. The poison's working its way out of their systems. They've got them on some kind of treatment – didn't catch all the medical terms, but the doctor seemed confident." He turned to me. "How about you? You disappeared pretty fast back there."

"Let's just say I feel significantly lighter now," I managed, remembering my desperate race through town. "Though probably not as light as Mayor Thompson will be after his extended bathroom retreat. Mrs. Thompson called the bakery twice looking for him – apparently he's not answering his phone."

"Can't imagine why," Shawn smirked. "Though I hear the bakery's considering naming that bathroom after him. Longest single occupancy in town history."

Robert's laugh carried a harsh edge. "Serves him right, way he's been strutting around lately with that new secretary of his. Did you hear about their 'business lunch' at Rose's yesterday? Three hours to discuss parking regulations."

Shawn shook his head. "Should've known Valentine's Day wouldn't pass quietly. This town hasn't had a normal holiday since you moved here, Jim."

"At least this one didn't involve falling Christmas trees," I said. "Though mass poisoning wasn't exactly the celebration we had in mind."

Robert's expression suddenly grew serious. "Speaking of poisoning... heard about Edison."

The mood shifted immediately, humor draining away like water down a drain. Shawn's face fell, his earlier amusement replaced by genuine grief.

"Yeah." His voice dropped lower, nearly lost in the hospital's ambient noise. "Good man, Edison. Bit unlucky with his ventures maybe, but he had heart. Used to come by the bar, talk about his latest investment ideas. Had this whole plan about renovating that old warehouse by the harbor, turning it into some kind of maritime museum. Still had that spark, you know? Even at his age."

A child's cry pierced the relative quiet, quickly hushed by a worried mother. Through the emergency department's automatic doors, I could see more people arriving from town. Word was spreading fast.

"Who do you think did it?" Robert asked, his voice barely above a whisper. The question we'd all been avoiding hung in the air between us. "I mean... Sophie..." He twisted his wedding ring nervously, a habit I'd noticed during our previous cases.

"Hard to believe," Shawn said softly, watching an elderly couple shuffle past, the woman supporting her clearly ill husband. "Sophie's different from Maggie. You can see it in how she treats people. How she runs the bakery." He paused, considering. "But then again, we all thought Maggie was different too. Until she wasn't."

"Let's not jump to conclusions," I said, though Maggie's ghost seemed to hover at the edges of the conversation. "We need to investigate properly. Find out exactly what happened. There could be more to this than we're seeing."

"But after Maggie..." Robert trailed off, his hands working against each other like he was trying to untangle a particularly stubborn knot. "You have to admit, it looks-"

A nurse appeared beside us, her feet silent on the linoleum floor. Her name tag read "Sarah," and her scrubs featured tiny teddy bears that seemed oddly cheerful given the circumstances. Looking at her auburn hair and kind eyes, I thought of my daughter. Sarah was about the same age – she'd probably be worried if she heard about mass poisonings in her father's quiet coastal town.

"Mr. Butterfield?" Her voice carried that particular mix of efficiency and compassion that good nurses seem to master. "You wanted to see them? Dr. Chen called ahead, mentioned you'd be coming."

I stood, perhaps too quickly. My stomach reminded me it wasn't entirely happy about sudden movements yet. "Are they awake?"

She shook her head, adjusting her clipboard. "Still unconscious, but stable. Their vital signs are good, and the blood work is encouraging. You can visit briefly – just try to keep your voices down. Room 112." Her expression softened slightly. "Don't worry about Ginger – we're treating him just like our other patients. Doctor Matthews has a soft spot for animals anyway, especially ones that help solve crimes. Says his daughter followed the Liam's case in the paper."

The hospital corridors carried that particular quiet that seems unique to medical facilities – not silence exactly, but a hush broken by steady beeps, distant conversations, and the squeak of cart wheels. The walls bore a fresh coat of mint green paint that probably seemed soothing to someone, somewhere. Fluorescent lights buzzed overhead, making everyone look slightly ill.

Room 112 sat halfway down the hall. The room number plaque had been polished recently, catching the afternoon light. Inside, the winter sunlight filtered through vertical blinds, creating stripes across two beds. The air carried that particular hospital scent – antiseptic mixed with something else, something that spoke of illness and healing all at once.

Emma occupied the bed near the window, her constellation dress somehow still twinkling faintly despite its wearer's unconscious state. Even in her sleep, her expression suggested she might be receiving cosmic predictions. Someone – probably Shawn – had rescued a few of her crystals from the bakery chaos, arranging them on the bedside table in what was probably a significant pattern. A particularly large rose quartz seemed to pulse gently in the striped sunlight, though that might have been my imagination.

Ginger lay curled on the other bed, his orange fur catching the striped sunlight. Medical equipment beeped steadily beside him, though someone had had the sense not to try attaching actual monitors. A small dish of what looked like spring water sat within easy reach, and an unopened tin of gourmet cat food waited nearby – clearly the staff had been briefed on their unusual patient's standards. They'd even provided a proper pillow, though Ginger had naturally chosen to ignore it in favor of curling into his own particular arrangement.

"He looks so peaceful," I said softly, moving closer to Ginger's bed. His whiskers twitched slightly in sleep, suggesting whatever dreams cats have. "Almost like he's just napping after solving another case."

"Emma too," Robert added from near the window. He adjusted the blinds slightly, letting in more light. "Though even unconscious she looks like she's about to announce a planetary alignment." He reached out to adjust one of her crystals, then thought better of it. "Probably shouldn't disturb the cosmic energy or whatever she calls it. Remember what happened last time someone moved her rose quartz?"

"The fortune-telling strike?" Shawn chuckled softly. "Three days of refusing to read anyone's future. Said the crystal alignments were too disturbed for accurate predictions."

"The doctors say the medication should help neutralize the poison," Sarah explained in a whisper, checking something on her clipboard. "Though they're still running tests to identify exactly what it was. We're keeping them comfortable while their bodies process it out."

Through the window, I could see snow beginning to fall again, adding another layer of white to the hospital grounds. A maintenance worker struggled with a stubborn snowblower near the parking lot, the machine's protests barely audible through the glass.

I watched Ginger's steady breathing, remembering our morning at Mrs. Henderson's, investigating her missing Valentine. Had that really been just hours ago? It felt like days had passed since we'd listened to her theories about international art thieves and suspicious minivans.

"I should have been there," I said, more to myself than the others. My hand rested on the bed rail, cold metal grounding me in the moment. "Instead of running off to-"

"To avoid dying of embarrassment in Sophie's bathroom?" Shawn finished with a slight smile. "While Mayor Thompson conducted his extended occupation? Pretty sure Ginger would understand."

"Besides," Robert added, "what could you have done? Carried them both while dealing with your own crisis? Sometimes even detectives need a bathroom break." His attempt at humor fell flat in the quiet room.

They had a point, but guilt gnawed at me anyway. My hands clenched into fists as I watched my partner sleep. Through the window, the maintenance worker had finally gotten the snowblower started, its muffled roar providing a counterpoint to the steady beeping of medical equipment.

Whoever had done this – whether it was Sophie following her sister's dark path or someone else entirely – they'd hurt people I cared about. Made me abandon Ginger when he needed me. The thought of Sophie potentially following Maggie's path seemed impossible, yet here we were again, surrounded by victims of another poisoning.

"We'll find who did this," I promised softly, watching Ginger's whiskers twitch in sleep. "And make sure they answer for it. No more poisonings in this town."

"Speaking of answering," Sarah said from the doorway, her teddy bear scrubs somehow managing to look both professional and apologetic. The bears seemed to dance slightly as she moved. "I'm sorry, but visiting hours are ending. They need to rest, and so do you by the look of it."

She was right – exhaustion pulled at me, a combination of the morning's events and whatever that poison had done to my system. But leaving Ginger felt wrong somehow, like abandoning him twice in one day.

"Go home," Sarah added more gently, her voice carrying that particular mix of kindness and authority that good nurses master. "Take some rest. We'll take good care of them, I promise."

I paused at the doorway, looking back at the unlikely pair – the eccentric fortune teller and the sarcastic cat, both peaceful in sleep despite everything that had happened. The striped sunlight painted them in alternating bands of light and shadow.

"I'll be back tomorrow," I promised. "And I'll figure out who did this. No matter what it takes."

The corridor's fluorescent lights hummed overhead as we walked away, their steady buzz mixing with the usual hospital sounds – distant conversations, squeaking wheels, the soft chime of an elevator arriving. Fresh snow drifted past the windows, the flakes dancing in the morning light. Somewhere in town, someone was probably feeling pretty pleased with themselves right now, thinking they'd managed a perfect crime.

They were wrong.

The elevator doors closed with a soft ding, carrying us back toward the lobby where more Valentine's Day victims waited. I thought about Sophie's face when the officers questioned her, about Brenda's methodical cleaning of fallen decorations, about all the little details that might mean nothing or everything. Time to start investigating properly.

As we passed the emergency department's sliding doors, I heard Chuck's voice drift out from where he still sat clutching his stomach: "What do you mean Thompson's still in the bakery bathroom? It's been two hours! Someone needs to do something about this!"

Mrs. Henderson's voice carried clearly from near the intake desk: "I told you all about those suspicious minivans! First Valentine cards, now poisonings – it's clearly an organized crime ring targeting small coastal towns. Barbara's cousin in Maine saw something very similar last month..."

Some mysteries, it seemed, would have to solve themselves. But the important ones – the ones involving unconscious friends and potentially murderous bakers – those would require proper detective work. And maybe some assistance from a certain sarcastic feline, once he decided to rejoin the conscious world.

I just hoped he'd forgive me for the part about being carried in Shawn's bar apron. Though given his standards for proper detective transport, I'd probably be hearing about the indignity of being "delivered like a bar snack" for months to come.

# Chapter 5

After leaving Shawn to handle the morning's alcohol delivery at the Salty Breeze and Robert to return to his waiting boat at the docks, I made my way back to Sophie's bakery. The late morning sun illuminated police tape fluttering in the winter breeze as I approached. The ambulances had departed, leaving only a few police cruisers and Miller's distinctive vehicle parked haphazardly near the entrance. Tire tracks in the fresh snow marked where the emergency vehicles had been, like scars on the pristine white surface.

Inside, the usual warm scent of fresh bread and pastries had been overtaken by the sharp odor of cleaning products. Sophie stood alone near the display cases, methodically wiping down surfaces that already gleamed. Her normally pristine apron bore evidence of the morning's chaos – spots of chocolate, streaks of food coloring, and what might have been tear stains. Two officers lounged near the entrance, putting more effort into appearing busy than actually investigating. Their notebooks remained conspicuously blank as they studied the ceiling with exaggerated interest.

Sophie looked up as I entered, and the relief on her face was painful to see. "Jim," she said softly, setting down her cleaning cloth. "Thank goodness. I was hoping you'd come back." Her voice carried the particular exhaustion that comes from holding oneself together through a crisis. "How's Ginger? And Emma?"

"Still unconscious, but the doctors say they're stable. The treatment seems to be working." I studied her face, noting the shadows under her eyes. "How are you holding up?"

"Honestly? I don't even know anymore." Her hands twisted the cleaning cloth absently. "One minute we're celebrating Valentine's Day, everything perfect, decorations just right... and the next..." She gestured helplessly at the chaos around us. "I keep thinking I'll wake up and find this was all some horrible dream."

"Where are Brenda and Mrs. Abernathy?"

Sophie moved to adjust a fallen display, though her movements seemed more about keeping her hands busy than actual cleaning now. "I sent them home after they gave their statements. This whole Valentine's celebration was my idea, my responsibility. There was no need for them to stay through this mess." She paused, swallowing hard. "Mrs. Abernathy was practically asleep on her feet after everything that happened. And Brenda... well, she was pretty shaken up. Never seen anything like this before."

"Tell me about the morning," I prompted gently. "Before everything went wrong. Walk me through it."

"It was perfect, Jim. Everything was just perfect." A ghost of enthusiasm crept into her voice. "We started at four AM – Mrs. Abernathy insisted on supervising the first batch of croissants. Said something about the pre-dawn air being essential for proper lamination. You know how she gets about proper technique."

Despite everything, a small smile touched her lips. "And Brenda – you should have seen her work with the decorations. She has this way with chocolate that's just amazing. We had such a good rhythm going – Mrs. Abernathy sharing techniques from her decades of experience, Brenda bringing fresh ideas about presentations." Pride crept into her voice despite the circumstances. "The chocolate work on those Valentine postcards? That was her design. She found this way to make the 'postmarks' look absolutely real."

"You worked well together then?"

"Better than I expected, honestly. I was worried at first, with Alice being away. But we just... clicked. Mrs. Abernathy showing us little tricks she's perfected over the years, Brenda suggesting new twists on traditional designs. I didn't even miss..." She caught herself. "I mean, with Alice away, I worried about managing everything, but we made such a great team."

"Speaking of Alice," I said carefully, watching her face. "Did anyone else have access to the bakery? Keys?"

"Just Alice, and she's been at her grandparents' for over two weeks now." Sophie's laugh held no humor. "Unless you think she drove hours in the middle of the night to poison Valentine's treats? That's the kind of theory Mrs. Henderson would love."

Mrs. Henderson's morning gossip surfaced in my memory. "What about your visitor yesterday? The man in the suit?"

Sophie's hands stilled on the display case. The silence stretched just a fraction too long before she answered. "You know how Mrs. Henderson is with her rumors. Next she'll be claiming he was a French pastry critic in disguise, here to steal my recipes."

Before I could press further, a familiar voice called from the kitchen: "Mayor Thompson! Need you to wrap it up in there. This place is about to become an official crime scene, and I don't want to explain to the whole town why the mayor is barricaded in the bathroom."

A muffled groan answered, followed by what might have been a mayoral attempt at dignity: "Just five more minutes!"

Miller emerged from the kitchen, his uniform already showing evidence of powdered sugar despite the early hour. One of his officers trailed behind him, carefully holding a plastic evidence bag that contained what looked like a crumpled receipt. Miller's expression carried the particular satisfaction of someone who thinks they've solved a complex case with minimal effort.

"Well, well," he announced, brushing donut residue from his shirt. "Looks like we can wrap this up nice and quick. Just like I thought – simple case, simple solution." He gestured to his officer. "Found this in the kitchen trash. Receipt for ten packs of laxatives, purchased yesterday. In Sophie's name."

Sophie's face went pale. "That's ridiculous! I never-"

"And this." Miller produced another evidence bag from his pocket with a flourish that sent more powdered sugar flying. Inside, I could see what appeared to be an empty vial. "Found it behind the flour bins. Traces of something that could explain our unconscious victims' symptoms. Lab will confirm, but I think we all know what happened here."

"If I did it," Sophie protested, her voice rising slightly, "why would I leave evidence in my own trash? That would be incredibly stupid!"

"Wouldn't be the first time," Miller said meaningfully. "Seems to run in the family. Your sister made the same mistake – left her receipt right where we could find it."

Sophie's hands clenched into fists at her sides. "I am not Maggie!"

"No?" Miller's eyebrows rose. "Different sister, same bakery, same M.O. Even left the evidence in the same place. Guess criminal genius doesn't run in the family either."

"This is absurd," Sophie said, but her voice had lost some of its fire. "I would never... all those people..." She gestured helplessly at the chaos around us. "Mr. Edison... he was a regular customer. Used to special order cookies for his great-grandchildren every Sunday – said they were the only thing that could get them to sit through dinner without complaining. Why would I..."

"People do strange things," Miller shrugged, clearly warming to his theory. "Pressure of running a business, living in your sister's shadow. Maybe you snapped. Wanted to make your own mark on the town's history. Though I gotta say," he added, brushing more sugar from his uniform, "poisoning people on Valentine's Day? That's cold, even by your family's standards."

"Sheriff," I tried to interject, "maybe we should-"

"Already got it figured, Butterfield," Miller cut me off. "No need for your amateur detective work this time. Got all the evidence right here." He patted the bags with satisfaction that sent another shower of sugar to the floor. "Receipt with her name, empty vial in her kitchen, witness statements about her strange behavior lately. That conversation with the mysterious man in the suit yesterday? Very suspicious."

Sophie's face, already pale, went almost white. The cleaning cloth slipped from her fingers, landing silently on the floor among the scattered Valentine's decorations.

"Need anything else for the paperwork?" Miller asked his officer, who was still diligently pretending to take notes.

"Just one thing, sir," the young man replied, flipping through his mostly empty notebook. "Should I file this under 'B' for 'Bakery Crime' or 'P' for 'Poisoning'? Or maybe 'V' for 'Valentine's Day Violations'?"

Miller considered this with far more seriousness than it deserved. "Better make it 'F' for 'Family Business.' Keep all those Brown sisters' cases together." He turned to Sophie, his expression shifting to what he probably thought was intimidating. "Speaking of family business – Sophie Brown, you're under arrest for multiple counts of assault through poisoning, and one count of manslaughter."

"This is ridiculous," Sophie protested as the younger officer moved to handcuff her. Her voice carried more exhaustion than anger now. "I didn't do this. Someone's setting me up – just like they tried to set Jim up for Peter's murder!"

"Save it for the judge," Miller said, already reaching for his phone – probably to order more donuts. "Martinez, get her out of here. And somebody tell Mayor Thompson he's got exactly two minutes before this becomes a sealed crime scene. Don't care if he has to crawl out that bathroom window."

As the officers led Sophie toward the door, she twisted to look back at me. "Jim! Please – you have to help! Someone's framing me, just like Maggie tried to frame you. You know what that's like!" Her voice cracked slightly. "Please find out who really did this!"

The door closed behind them with a finality that seemed too ordinary for the moment. Through the window, I watched as the officers helped Sophie into a patrol car, her normally confident posture diminished by handcuffs and circumstance. The late morning sun caught her face just before she ducked into the vehicle – she looked lost, confused, but not guilty. Then again, Maggie had looked innocent too, right up until she tried to kill me in my living room.

Miller emerged from giving Thompson his ultimatum, brushing what looked like fresh powdered sugar from his sleeve. "Don't even think about investigating this one, Butterfield," he said, his voice carrying the particular authority of someone who's afraid of extra paperwork. "Got this all wrapped up nice and neat. No loose ends, no complicated theories. Just a simple case of history repeating itself."

He paused at the door, then added with what he probably thought was kindness: "Look, I know you want to believe the best of people. But sometimes the simple answer is the right one. One sister opens a bakery and poisons customers, then the other does the same thing. Must run in the family."

The door closed behind him with a gentle chime that seemed inappropriate for the moment. I stood alone in the bakery, surrounded by the wreckage of what should have been a simple celebration. Crushed paper hearts and scattered rose petals covered the floor like evidence of shattered dreams. Through the window, I could see Miller's car pulling away, Sophie's pale face visible in the back seat.

A muffled groan from the bathroom reminded me that at least one victim of the morning's events remained. "Mayor Thompson?" I called out. "Miller's gone. But you really should-"

"Just five more minutes!" came the weak reply. "Maybe ten. Fifteen at most. Unless..." Another groan. "Is there any chance of bathroom delivery service in this town?"

I left him to his extended mayoral duties and walked slowly around the bakery, trying to see it as a crime scene rather than a place I'd come to know well. The kitchen still carried the warm scent of fresh-baked goods, mixed now with cleaning products and the particular sadness of abandoned celebrations. Half-finished Valentine's displays sat like accusations on every surface.

Had Sophie really done this? Followed in her sister's footsteps? The evidence seemed damning – the receipt, the vial, her strange behavior lately. But something felt off about it all. Too neat, too convenient. Like someone had carefully arranged all the pieces to tell a specific story.

The question was: what was the real story? And who was really telling it?

Through the window, I could see Mrs. Henderson had already gathered a small crowd of observers across the street. Her hands moved animatedly as she shared her theories, probably involving international pastry spies and mysterious minivans with foreign license plates. But for once, I wondered if she might have inadvertently stumbled onto something important. That man in the suit Sophie had been seen talking to – why did she react so strongly when I mentioned him?

A sudden crash from the bathroom made me jump. "Everything okay in there, Mayor?"

"Fine! Everything's fine!" His voice carried a mixture of embarrassment and desperation. "Just... rearranging some fixtures. For civic improvement purposes. Though if anyone's heading to the hardware store, we might need a new toilet paper holder. And possibly a new sink."

I left him to his civic improvements and continued my inspection of the bakery. The morning sun streamed through the windows, catching the sugar scattered across the floor like evidence of broken dreams. Each crystalline grain seemed to hold a fragment of what this day should have been – celebrations and joy, not poisonings and arrests.

The question that kept nagging at me: why would Sophie leave such obvious evidence? The receipt in her own name, the vial barely hidden? It seemed too careless for someone who measured ingredients down to the gram. Then again, we'd thought the same about Maggie, and look how that turned out.

A final, particularly distressing sound emerged from the bathroom, followed by the mayor's voice: "Is there any chance the town budget covers emergency plumbing? Asking for a friend. A friend who might have just created a situation that requires professional intervention."

I probably should have stayed to help deal with the mayor's plumbing crisis. But Sophie's words kept echoing in my mind: *"Someone's framing me, just like Maggie tried to frame you."* She was right about one thing – I did know what that felt like. The question was: could I trust her? Or was this just another Brown sister following a dark family tradition?

Only one way to find out.

As I left the bakery, snowflakes had begun to fall again. Mrs. Henderson's voice carried across the street: "And then the mysterious man in the suit was seen entering a minivan with foreign plates! Barbara's cousin in Maine saw something very similar right before that mysterious croissant incident last month..."

For once, I found myself hoping she might actually be onto something. Because the alternative – that Sophie had simply followed her sister's murderous path – seemed too tragic to contemplate.

The morning that had started with a missing Valentine card had somehow evolved into something much more mysterious. But one thing was certain: despite Miller's warnings, despite the seeming simplicity of his solution, I had to find out what really happened. I owed that much to Emma, to Ginger, to everyone who'd been hurt today.

Valentine's Day in Oceanview Cove had turned out exactly as complicated as our town's holidays usually did. But this time, the stakes felt even higher. Because somewhere behind all the obvious clues and easy answers lurked a truth that someone had gone to great lengths to hide.

Time to start digging.

# Chapter 6

The afternoon winter sun slanted across Mrs. Abernathy's front porch as I approached, my footsteps crunching in the fresh snow. The well-maintained Victorian home stood in stark contrast to Mrs. Henderson's controlled chaos down the street. Every shutter hung perfectly straight, every window gleamed, and even the icicles seemed to have arranged themselves with mathematical precision. The winter birds at her feeders appeared to have absorbed some of her standards – they took turns at the perches with almost choreographed politeness.

A note fluttered on the front door, held in place by a brass tack that matched the door's antique hardware perfectly in both color and patina. Mrs. Abernathy's precise handwriting – the kind that probably made calligraphers weep with envy – informed any visitors that she had gone to the library and would return in the evening. The paper itself appeared to be artisanal stationery with a subtle watermark, because of course Mrs. Abernathy wouldn't leave notes on anything less than perfection.

"Only Mrs. Abernathy would coordinate her emergency notes with her door fixtures," I muttered, studying the elegant script. "I notice she's arranged the text with perfect margins. Even her hasty notes put my best handwriting to shame."

The library. In all my months in Oceanview Cove, solving murders and holiday-themed crimes, I'd somehow never visited the one place that should have felt most like home. The thought brought a wave of guilt – Martha would have been disappointed in me for neglecting my roots. She used to tease me about having book dust in my veins instead of blood.

The Oceanview Cove Public Library occupied a stately brick building near the town center, its weathered cornerstone declaring it had been serving the community since 1892. Wide stone steps, worn smooth by generations of readers' feet, led to wooden doors that bore the patina of countless hands. The afternoon light caught the leaded glass windows, creating patterns that danced across the worn steps like bookmarks dropped by hurrying patrons.

Inside, the familiar scent of books and wood polish wrapped around me like a welcome embrace. The high ceilings carried whispered conversations up into shadowed rafters, while brass reading lamps cast pools of warm light across oak tables that could have been there since opening day. A few ancient computers huddled in one corner, looking somewhat apologetic about their modern intrusion into this temple of traditional learning. Their screensavers displayed floating books, as if trying to prove they understood their environment.

"At least these computers look properly intimidated by their surroundings," I mused, noting how even the electrical cords seemed to try hiding themselves behind classical literature.

A young couple browsed the fiction section, their heads bent close together as they discussed book choices in whispered tones that carried the particular reverence unique to libraries. She held what appeared to be a well-worn Jane Austen, while he balanced a stack of Kurt Vonnegut. Their gentle debate about literary merits versus readability drifted across the quiet space.

The sight triggered a rush of memory – Martha used to visit my library after her government job, and we'd spend hours choosing our evening reading material. We had our own shorthand for recommendations: one tap on a spine meant "maybe," two meant "definitely," and three meant "this one will keep you up all night." She always teased me about my preference for mysteries, claiming I was doing professional research even then.

The library's layout felt familiar despite my first visit – books have their own geography that transcends individual buildings. I moved past Biography (arranged chronologically rather than alphabetically, suggesting a traditionalist librarian), where Teddy Roosevelt seemed to glare at me from several spines at once. Skirted the edge of Reference (where a teenager appeared to be trying to defeat writer's block through sheer force of will and excessive coffee consumption), and found myself in the Cookbook section.

Mrs. Abernathy stood amid the culinary texts like a captain on her bridge, frantically flipping through what appeared to be an ancient tome of French pastry. Her usually perfect posture had wilted slightly, and her reading glasses had slipped to the very tip of her nose. She'd changed out of her flour-dusted bakery clothes into the cardigan that featured delicate embroidered cookies around the collar – each one stitched with the same precision she demanded in her baking. She muttered something that sounded suspiciously like "proportions" and "proper temperature variations" as she turned pages with increasing urgency.

"Mrs. Abernathy?"

She didn't respond, too absorbed in her desperate research. Her fingers traced recipe lines with the intensity of someone searching sacred texts for hidden meaning. A small pile of discarded books lay beside her, their spines suggesting a thorough investigation of everything from basic baking chemistry to advanced French techniques.

"Mrs. Abernathy?" I tried again, touching her shoulder gently.

She startled so violently that several recipe cards fluttered from between the book's pages, scattering across the floor like autumn leaves. One landed in front of a passing student who, upon seeing Mrs. Abernathy's name, carefully placed it on a nearby table and backed away slowly –

her reputation for exactitude apparently extended beyond baking.

"Mr. Butterfield! Oh goodness, you gave me quite a fright." She pressed one hand to her chest, her other still clutching the book like a lifeline. "I suppose I was rather focused on my research. These French measurements can be so particular – did you know they have seventeen different words for types of cream?"

I helped her gather the escaped recipe cards, noting that each one was written in the same precise handwriting that had graced the front door note. The cards themselves appeared to be from a special collection – each one watermarked with a small whisk design.

"What exactly are you researching?" I asked, noticing how some of the recipes had been annotated with multiple colors of ink, each shade presumably indicating a different level of culinary concern.

Her hands twisted together, a gesture so unlike her usual composed demeanor that it was almost shocking. The movement betrayed her distress, making her seem suddenly vulnerable despite her usual precision and control.

"I had to check – had to be certain. All those people ill, poor Mr. Edison..." She swallowed hard, her voice carrying the particular strain of someone trying very hard to maintain composure. "I keep thinking, what if I made a mistake? Mixed up ingredients, confused measurements? At my age, it's possible to-" She gestured helplessly at the pile of reference books. "I've been through every recipe three times, checking proportions, temperatures, possible chemical reactions..."

"Did you use any laxatives in your recipes?" I interrupted gently. "Or unknown substances that cause unconsciousness?"

"What? No! Of course not!" Her indignation briefly overcame her worry, making her stand straighter. The cookbook she held became a shield of culinary righteousness. "I would never- I mean, the very idea- wait." Understanding dawned in her eyes like the first morning light hitting her perfectly arranged kitchen. "You mean..."

I nodded. "Dr. Chen already identified the substances involved. Whatever caused this, it wasn't your recipes."

The tension visibly drained from her shoulders. She carefully closed the ancient pastry tome, smoothing its worn cover with hands that had finally stopped shaking. The book seemed to lean into her touch, like even it knew she'd never betray proper baking procedures.

"Oh thank goodness. I've been going through every recipe, every measurement, wondering if..." She trailed off, suddenly looking around the library's hushed interior. "Oh dear, where has Mr. Whiskers gotten to? I left him right here on this couch, looking quite regal despite his discomfort."

An empty couch nearby bore a distinct impression in its cushion, along with a few silver hairs that suggested recent feline occupation.

"He's still having some... digestive issues," Mrs. Abernathy explained delicately, peering around a nearby shelf of medieval cooking techniques. "Probably stepped outside for another... well." Her cheeks colored slightly. "Poor dear refuses to use a litter box. Apparently it's beneath his dignity. Though I suspect even his standards for proper facilities may have temporarily lowered given the circumstances."

We settled onto the couch, the aged leather creaking softly beneath us. The afternoon light filtered through tall windows creating a peaceful atmosphere that seemed at odds with our conversation's gravity. Dust motes danced in the golden beams, looking rather like sugar that had decorated Sophie's Valentine's treats just hours ago.

"But Mr. Butterfield," she said suddenly, adjusting her glasses with the particular precision she usually reserved for frosting placement. "Here I am worrying about recipes when I haven't even asked – how are you? And Ginger and Emma? I've been so focused on checking measurements that I completely forgot my manners. My grandmother would be appalled."

I filled her in on their conditions, watching how her hands automatically smoothed nonexistent wrinkles from her skirt as she listened. The gesture reminded me of Sophie's nervous apron-twisting earlier. Her fingers traced the embroidered cookies on her cardigan as if seeking comfort in their familiar patterns.

"Now," I said, keeping my voice low in deference to our location, "tell me about this morning. Everything you remember."

Her account aligned perfectly with Sophie's earlier description – the pre-dawn baking, the careful preparation of special treats, the division of labor among the three of them. Her words carried the particular precision of someone used to exact measurements, occasionally pausing to correct tiny details like the exact minute she arrived or the specific temperature of the ovens.

"We each had our specialties," she explained, absently adjusting a slightly crooked table lamp nearby. A small stack of early reader books looked dangerously close to toppling, so she straightened those too. "Sophie focused on the croissants – she's really mastered the lamination technique, though I still think she could benefit from a slightly longer proof time. Just three more minutes would achieve optimal butter distribution." Her hands sketched pastry layers in the air. "I handled the cookies, of course. And Brenda..." A small frown creased her forehead. "Well, her work with chocolate is really quite remarkable. Those Valentine postcard designs were absolutely inspired. Though her tempering technique could use some refinement."

"Did you notice anything unusual? Any strange behavior?"

She considered this, her hands now automatically straightening the stack of cookbooks on a nearby table.

One particularly ancient volume about bread making seemed to resist her organizational efforts, its worn spine refusing to align with its neighbors.

"Sophie seemed a bit nervous, but that's understandable – she wanted everything to be perfect. First major celebration since taking over the bakery." She paused, then added more quietly, "First chance to really step out of Maggie's shadow, I suppose."

"What about the man in the suit? Mrs. Henderson mentioned seeing Sophie talking to someone last night."

The cookbooks now properly aligned (except for the rebellious bread volume), Mrs. Abernathy's hands moved to adjust her already perfect collar. The embroidered cookies danced under her nervous fingers.

"For once, Mrs. Henderson's gossip is accurate. I saw it myself yesterday evening, after I'd left the bakery. A car pulled up – one of those sleek modern things that look more like spaceships than proper automobiles. All black and tinted windows." She shook her head slightly, clearly disapproving of such automotive ostentation. "A man got out, very well-dressed. Custom suit, I'd say – the cut was too perfect for off-the-rack. Started talking to Sophie rather intently. She seemed... uncomfortable."

A student passing nearby paused to return a book to its shelf, and Mrs. Abernathy waited until they moved on before continuing in a lower voice.

"I was too far to hear anything, of course. Asked Sophie about it this morning, but she just mumbled something about an old acquaintance and changed the subject. Nearly burned a batch of macarons right after – most unlike her. Sophie never burns anything."

I made a mental note to track down this mysterious visitor. Someone well-dressed enough to catch Mrs. Abernathy's attention, making Sophie nervous enough to burn pastries – that couldn't be coincidence. Not today of all days.

"Mrs. Henderson also mentioned something about you buying exotic spices in the city recently," I said. "Secret late-night shopping trips?"

Mrs. Abernathy chuckled, shaking her head. "That woman's rumors are only ever half-true. I have been going to the city, but hardly in secret. Some ingredients simply can't be found in Oceanview Cove, and I refuse to compromise on quality for my cookies. Though I'm sure by next week she'll have me involved in an international spice-smuggling ring."

I switched topics, remembering something Sophie had mentioned at the Salty Breeze after our last case. "Brenda was one of your students, wasn't she?"

"Oh yes," she nodded, finally letting her hands rest in her lap, though they still twitched occasionally toward crooked books. "One of my first, actually. Must have been... oh, thirty years ago now? She was just a girl, still in middle school. Had real passion for baking, but..." She trailed off, choosing her words carefully like selecting the perfect ingredient.

"But?" I prompted gently.

"Well, she was rather impatient. Wanted everything to happen faster – faster learning, faster success. Didn't quite understand that some things can't be rushed." Mrs. Abernathy's hands returned to straightening things, this time targeting a stack of library bookmarks that probably hadn't been touched in months. "Proper pastry takes time, you know. You can't hurry lamination or force dough to rise before it's ready. It's like trying to make spring come early – nature has its own schedule."

She sighed, finally abandoning the bookmarks. "I remember once she tried to speed up a proofing process using a hair dryer. The results were... not optimal. But the local birds enjoyed the results of that particular experiment."

That caught my interest. "Did she ever try to open her own bakery?"

"She wanted to. Even approached Maggie about being an assistant, learning the business side of things. But Maggie..." Mrs. Abernathy's mouth tightened slightly, her expression suggesting memories better left undisturbed. "Well, Maggie preferred to work alone. Said something rather unkind about Brenda's chocolate tempering technique, as I recall."

A library cart squeaked past, pushed by a young woman who seemed determined to reshelve books as quietly as possible. The sound still made Mrs. Abernathy wince slightly.

"Where did Brenda work before this? I don't remember seeing her around town."

"Oh, she's had various jobs – cashier, waitress, that sort of thing." Mrs. Abernathy's hands found a slightly dusty shelf edge and were absently cleaning it with her handkerchief. "Been working in Rocky Point this past year, I believe. The Silver Spoon Diner, if I remember correctly. That's probably why you haven't seen her, even though she lives right here in town. Though I did hear her pastry case displays were always particularly artistic."

Through the tall library windows, I could see snow beginning to fall again. The flakes danced in the afternoon light like sugar sifted from one of Mrs. Abernathy's precision sieves.

I leaned forward slightly. "Speaking of which – where exactly does she live? I'd like to talk to her, see if she noticed anything unusual at the bakery. After all, she's been working with Sophie for two weeks now."

Mrs. Abernathy provided the address – a small house on Cedar Street, not far from the harbor. I knew the area, thankfully. No need to battle my technological nemesis for GPS guidance this time. Though knowing my luck with technology, the phone would probably try to direct me to Cedar Rapids, Iowa.

"Thank you," I said, standing. The leather couch protested the movement with a soft creak that earned a disapproving glance from a passing librarian. "This has been very helpful."

She looked up at me, worry creasing her forehead again. The embroidered cookies on her collar seemed to droop slightly, sharing her concern. "I do hope Ginger and Emma recover quickly. And Mr. Butterfield?" Her voice caught slightly. "I am sorry about all of this. Even if it wasn't my recipes..."

"It wasn't your fault," I assured her firmly. "Someone did this deliberately. We just need to figure out who."

As I walked through the library's front doors, the afternoon light had taken on the particular golden quality that suggests approaching evening. The air carried the sharp bite of winter and the promise of more snow.

A distinct sound of distress from behind a nearby ornamental bush caught my attention, followed by what could only be described as feline complaints about indignity and proper facilities.

"I do hope that bush survives Mr. Whiskers's gastrointestinal crisis," I muttered.

Some mysteries, it seemed, solved themselves rather messily. But the important ones – the ones involving poisoned friends and framed bakers – those required more careful investigation.

Time to pay Brenda a visit, and hopefully find some answers that didn't involve compromised shrubbery.

# Chapter 7

Cedar Street's small houses huddled against the winter afternoon, their snow-frosted roofs and steamy windows suggesting cozy warmth within. Unlike Mrs. Abernathy's proudly maintained Victorian or Mrs. Henderson's cheerfully chaotic dwelling, Brenda's Cape Cod seemed to duck its head, as if asking forgiveness for its existence. The paint had surrendered to weather in places, and one shutter appeared to be rethinking its life choices, hanging at a rebellious angle.

A faded red Volkswagen Beetle occupied the narrow driveway, its bumper adorned with a single sticker that read "Life is Sweet When You're Baking." The car had clearly seen better days but wore its age with stubborn dignity, much like an elderly aunt who refuses to admit she needs reading glasses.

The front yard revealed someone's determined battle with nature – herb planters arranged with geometric precision fought against winter's grip, their markers labeled in careful calligraphy. A dormant vegetable patch waited beneath the snow, its borders outlined with the same mathematical exactness as a blueprint. Wind chimes fashioned from old cookie cutters and measuring spoons created metallic music that somehow managed to sound both welcoming and slightly desperate.

The porch steps voiced their opinion about visitors with a series of complaining creaks. The welcome mat depicted rolling pins and whisks engaged in what appeared to be some kind of culinary dance number, though time had reduced their enthusiasm to faded suggestions of movement.

My knock echoed in the winter quiet. Through the door's decorative window, I caught glimpses of movement – someone approaching with footsteps that seemed to count beats, like a metronome marking time. The door opened to reveal Brenda, still in her work clothes minus the apron. Her dark hair remained captured in its neat bun, though a few strands had staged a successful escape attempt. A smudge of flour decorated one cheek like artistic punctuation.

"Mr. Butterfield!" Her surprise seemed genuine, though her hands immediately began straightening her already straight collar. "How are you feeling? And Ginger – any news from the hospital?"

"I'm managing," I assured her. "Though I wouldn't recommend trying to break Mayor Thompson's bathroom occupation record. Ginger's in good hands – they're treating him just like their human patients."

"Such a terrible thing to happen," she said quietly, then brightened slightly. "Please, come in. I just pulled my anxiety cookies from the oven. Some people stress-eat – I stress-bake. Second batch since I got home, if we're counting. Which I am, because proper documentation is essential in baking. Helps keep my mind off... well, everything."

The interior of Brenda's house revealed someone caught between reality and aspiration. Her small living room had surrendered its traditional purpose to become a test kitchen, with a professional stand mixer occupying a counter built to its exact specifications. The measurement of the counter's height had likely involved advanced calculus and possibly a protractor.

Cookbooks lined custom shelves in arrangements that would have made a library scientist weep with joy. They were categorized not just by type but by sub-categories that included "Failed Attempts To Recreate" and "Almost But Not Quite Perfect Yet." Post-it notes protruded from their pages like colorful tongues, each one marked with precise observations and timestamps.

"Quite the collection," I noted, scanning titles that ranged from basic techniques to advanced French pastry.

"Most of these were my mother's," Brenda said, her fingers unconsciously aligning a measuring cup that had dared to face three degrees off center. "She loved baking too. Started teaching me when I could barely reach the counter." Her voice softened. "Lost her and dad eight years ago. Car accident on black ice. Random chance and physics conspiring to..." She trailed off, squaring her shoulders with mechanical precision.

"I'm sorry," I said quietly.

"It's fine. Well, not fine, but..." She gestured around the kitchen. "I inherited the house, the books, everything. Started throwing myself into baking after that. Some people get cats when they're lonely – I perfect recipes. Eight hundred and forty-seven attempts at the same chocolate chip cookie recipe so far. I maintain a spreadsheet."

The kitchen itself reflected her dedication. A professional convection oven that probably required a small loan stood next to a refrigerator old enough to vote. Specialized baking tools hung on the walls in patterns that suggested each placement had been measured with a ruler. The arrangements created shapes – hearts, stars, rolling pins – though whether this was intentional or a side effect of obsessive organization remained unclear.

"Tea?" she offered, already moving toward a kettle that gleamed with recent polishing. "Just got this fascinating blend that's supposed to complement shortbread perfectly. Though their recommended steeping time is clearly wrong – I've run tests. Thirty-seven seconds less produces optimal results. I have a chart somewhere..."

"Tea would be nice," I said, settling into a kitchen chair that had witnessed decades of family meals. The wood bore smooth patches that mapped generations of elbows and shifting positions. A plate of cookies appeared before me with the sudden precision of a magic trick. Each one could have been a geometry lesson in circular perfection.

A stack of index cards sat nearby, each filled with what appeared to be baking formulas rather than recipes. One read "Cookie Spreading Rate vs. Room Temperature: A Longitudinal Study." Brenda noticed my glance and immediately moved to align the stack's edges with mathematical precision.

"Mrs. Abernathy mentioned you were one of her first students," I said, accepting tea in a mug whose cartoon rolling pins seemed slightly manic in their cheerfulness.

"Thirty years, two months, and approximately fourteen days ago," Brenda nodded, her own mug featuring dancing cupcakes with eerily synchronized movements. She settled into a chair that had been placed at what was probably a carefully calculated angle. "I drove her absolutely crazy, I'm sure. Always trying to find shortcuts, optimize processes. That hair dryer incident with the proofing dough – I maintain that my hypothesis about accelerated yeast activation was sound, even if the execution needed refinement."

I tried one of the cookies. It was perfect – the kind of perfect that comes from someone who might own calipers specifically for measuring cookie thickness. The flavor balance suggested hours of testing different butter-to-sugar ratios.

My eyes were drawn to a wall covered in diagrams and plans. "Brenda's Sweet Dreams Bakery" evolved through various iterations, each more detailed than the last. The most recent version included precise measurements down to the millimeter, with notes about optimal display case angles.

"Your own bakery?" I asked.

"The dream that keeps me up until 3 AM practicing piping techniques," she smiled. "Four attempts, twelve loan applications, and twenty-seven rejection letters," she added. Her hands wrapped around the mug in a grip that suggested the dancing cupcakes might need rescuing. "Banks want collateral, experience, proven track records. Hard to prove yourself when no one will give you a chance."

She paused to adjust a cookie that had rotated approximately two degrees during our conversation. "Even tried apprenticing with Maggie. That was... educational. Did you know there are seventeen different ways to criticize someone's chocolate tempering technique? She found all of them. In one afternoon."

"Must have been difficult," I said, watching how her fingers kept returning to adjust things – the angle of a spoon, the spacing between mugs, the alignment of napkins with the table edge.

"The past exists as historical data points," she replied, but her knuckles whitened slightly around her mug. One of the dancing cupcakes appeared to be crying. "Though when Sophie hired me to fill in for Alice... well, let's just say my spreadsheet of career satisfaction metrics showed a statistically significant improvement."

Steam curled from our mugs in precise spirals that Brenda's eyes seemed to measure. The wall clock ticked with metronomic precision, each second marked like data points in an experiment. Outside, snow fell in patterns that she probably wished she could organize.

"How has it been, working with them both?"

"Wonderful, actually," she responded, rising to remove another batch of cookies with practiced movements. "Sophie's so different from other bakery owners I've worked for in other towns – she actually listens to ideas. And Mrs. Abernathy..." She gestured toward her cookbook collection with clear admiration. "Well, there's a reason she's the town's baking expert."

"Those Valentine's postcard designs were impressive," I noted, watching how she placed each cookie on the cooling rack with careful precision.

"Thank you. Took thirty-two attempts to get the chocolate just right," she nodded, adjusting the spacing between cookies.

"Did you notice anything unusual at the bakery?" I asked. "Before today's events, I mean."

Her hands stilled briefly. "Actually, yes. Sophie's been acting strange lately."

She began transferring cooled cookies to a plate. "Those notifications on her phone always made her nervous. She'd rush off to her office and come back looking worried."

"And then there was that man in the suit," Brenda continued, pausing to check the cookies' arrangement. "Their conversations seemed intense."

"You saw these meetings?"

"Three times exactly. Always after seven-thirty, when we'd closed for the day. Sophie always seemed anxious around him." She adjusted a slightly misaligned cookie. "At first I thought maybe it was a secret boyfriend or something. But it felt... different. More complicated. I never heard what they were talking about – I was already heading home those times. Just saw them through the bakery windows as I left."

The kitchen had grown darker as we talked. Brenda moved to adjust the lighting.

"Anything else unusual?" I asked, watching as she straightened an already-perfect dish towel.

"Well, she started taking phone calls outside in the cold. And she was always hiding papers when anyone came into her office. And yesterday..." She paused in her tidying, though her fingers twitched toward a crooked spoon.

"Yesterday?"

"I forgot my phone at the bakery, came back to get it. Heard voices from her office – sounded like quite an argument." Her hands resumed their adjusting. "When I mentioned it this morning, she said she'd been alone. Why would she lie about that? That man in the suit's car was right there in front of the bakery entrance."

The snow outside had intensified, adding another variable to the winter evening's equation. Brenda's small yard was transforming into a blank canvas of white, though I noticed her eyes measuring the depth accumulation with unusual intensity.

"There's something else you should know," I said. "The police arrested Sophie after you went home. They found evidence in her office – receipt for one of the substances used in the poisoning, an empty vial behind the flour bins."

Brenda's hands froze in their endless adjusting. "Arrested? But that's impossible. Sophie would never..." She shook her head, though I noticed her movements remained carefully controlled. "I should visit her at the station. Yes, first thing tomorrow – I have several batches of experimental recipes that require precise timing..."

I studied her face as she spoke. Her shock seemed genuine, but her lack of urgency felt oddly calculated. Still, she'd given me plenty to think about – especially regarding Sophie's secretive behavior. There wasn't much more I could learn here.

"Thank you," I said, standing. The chair legs scraped against the linoleum in a way that made her wince slightly. "You've been extremely helpful."

"Of course," she replied, already wrapping cookies. The wax paper creased at perfect angles. "Take these with you. And please, let me know if you need anything else." She presented the package with careful movements. "After all,

Sophie gave me such a wonderful opportunity. I really should visit her soon. Once I've finished documenting these test batches."

The porch light illuminated the snow with scientific accuracy as I left. Brenda's Beetle had accumulated exactly 1.3 inches of snow, or at least that's how she'd probably measure it. Her yard had become a study in winter precipitation patterns, each snowflake adding to data that she seemed to collect even unconsciously.

Walking through the snowy evening, something about our conversation nagged at me like an imperfect measurement. Brenda's responses had been precise – too precise, like someone who'd measured every word before speaking. Her helpfulness felt calculated, plotted on some internal graph of appropriate social interactions. But was it the mask of someone hiding darker variables, or simply the nature of a person who counted everything, even her own heartbeats?

I found myself missing Ginger's wit – he would have had some sardonic observation about Brenda's precise measurements of life, or a clever insight about her carefully controlled reactions. More than his sarcasm, I missed his ability to see through people's facades, to catch the small details I might overlook. Together we would have made sense of all this, but now I had to piece together this puzzle alone.

Through windows along the street, families gathered for dinner in scenes that defied Brenda's precise measurements. Her solitary kitchen, for all its professional equipment and careful organization, had felt more like a laboratory than a home. Everything arranged with mathematical perfection, measuring every aspect of life except perhaps happiness itself.

But Sophie hadn't been entirely forthcoming either. The mysterious suit-wearing visitor, the suspicious phone notifications, papers hidden from view – if Sophie wanted me to investigate, she needed to start being honest. The Valentine's Day poisoning had left more questions than answers, each one demanding closer examination.

Evening had settled fully over Oceanview Cove now, transforming the streets into quiet passages between pools of lamplight. Most people had retreated indoors, leaving only occasional footprints in the fresh snow to mark their passing.

The Valentine's Day poisoning had shaken our small town's foundation, leaving cracks in the surface of what we thought we knew about each other. Now it was just a matter of following those cracks to their source, wherever – or whoever – that might lead to.

The police station waited ahead, its lights promising answers but probably holding only more questions. Time to see what Sophie had to say about mysterious men in suits and her secret phone calls.

# Chapter 8

Evening shadows filled the police station as I entered, the usual bustle of day shift replaced by distant ringing phones and muffled conversations. The duty roster board listed Officer Jones for night shift, though someone had added a small coffee stain beside his name that looked suspiciously intentional. A distinct aroma of donuts lingered in the air, mixing with stale coffee and a particular blend of cleaning supplies that seemed unique to small-town law enforcement.

Miller sat behind his fortress of paperwork, surrounded by the archaeological evidence of a day spent actively avoiding actual police work. An empty donut box perched precariously atop what appeared to be last month's parking violations, its cheerful logo a reminder that he'd pointedly avoided Sophie's bakery in favor of Dunkin'. His computer screen displayed what looked suspiciously like his fifth attempt at solitaire, though he quickly minimized it when he noticed me.

"Butterfield!" He straightened, sending a small avalanche of powdered sugar cascading onto his already dusted uniform. A half-eaten jelly donut lay forgotten on a stack of "urgent" paperwork that probably hadn't been urgent since last summer. "Didn't I specifically warn you about investigating this case?"

"Actually," I said carefully, noting how his hand moved protectively toward a manila folder on his desk, "I'm here to look Sophie in the eyes. Get her confession." I channeled my best impression of his own dramatic police work. "How dare she follow Maggie's footsteps and poison innocent people on Valentine's Day?"

Miller's eyebrows shot up so high they threatened to join his receding hairline. A forgotten bit of donut icing clung to his mustache like edible evidence of his day's primary activity.

"What made you finally see reason?" Miller asked, wiping powdered sugar from his chin.

"Let's just say I realized the Brown sisters don't change," I replied with deliberate weariness. "Sometimes you have to face hard truths."

Miller checked his watch – one of those digital models that probably came free with a value meal, its display slightly clouded from what looked like more sugar deposits.

"Ten minutes," he declared, already inching his mouse toward the minimized solitaire game. A stack of reports labeled "Filing Priority: Eventual" teetered dangerously near his elbow. "Some of us have actual police work to do."

"Like organizing your donut loyalty card collection?" I couldn't help asking, eyeing the stack of partially stamped cards spilling from his desk drawer.

His glare might have been more effective without the icing accessory. "Nine minutes, Butterfield. And I'll have you know those cards are arranged by frosting type."

The holding cells occupied a small area past Miller's desk, separated from the main office by a door whose hinges protested any movement with the enthusiasm of ancient metalwork forced to continue working past retirement. The sound echoed off concrete walls painted an institutional shade of green that somehow managed to be both aggressively boring and vaguely nauseating. A small sign announced "Cell Block A" though the lack of a Cell Block B suggested someone's optimistic view of small-town crime rates.

Sophie sat alone in the first cell, perched on the edge of a narrow cot whose mattress had probably witnessed the station's founding. The harsh overhead lighting did her no favors, emphasizing the worry lines around her eyes and the flour dust that still clung to her clothes like memories of the morning's chaos. Her usually perfect posture had wilted slightly, though she straightened when she saw me – the instinctive reaction of someone used to maintaining appearances even in crisis.

"Jim! Thank goodness." Relief flooded her face, chasing away some of the harsh shadows. "I knew you'd believe I was innocent."

"Actually," I said, settling onto a wooden chair that creaked ominously, "I still have my doubts."

Her face fell faster than an underbaked soufflé. The cell's fluorescent light flickered dramatically, as if the electrical system had decided to provide mood lighting for interrogations.

"If you want my help," I continued, shifting on the chair, "you need to be completely honest. No convenient omissions, no carefully edited versions of events. Because right now? The evidence isn't painting a flattering picture."

She nodded slowly, her hands twisting in her lap. A distant phone rang three times before falling silent, its echo hanging in the charged air between us.

"Brenda mentioned some interesting behavior lately," I said, watching her face. "Phone notifications that made you nervous. Papers hidden in your office." I paused as another phone started ringing somewhere in the building. "And let's not forget your mysterious visitor in the expertly tailored suit."

Sophie's head snapped up. "How did you-"

"Mrs. Abernathy. Brenda." I smiled slightly. "And of course, Mrs. Henderson, though her version involved a French pastry critic in disguise scouting small-town bakeries for talented bakers."

Through the small, high window, I could see snow still falling, each flake caught in the security light like sugar sifted from heaven's own kitchen. The effect would have been peaceful if not for our surroundings and the gravity of the situation.

"If you want me to walk away," I said into the growing quiet, "just keep deflecting. But right now, none of this paints a picture of innocence."

Sophie was quiet for so long I thought she might have decided to take that option. Finally, she spoke, her voice barely above a whisper: "It's about Maggie."

The name dropped into the space between us like a stone into still water. Even the flickering light seemed to pause, as if listening.

"She's been writing to me," Sophie continued, her hands still working against each other. "For the past month. Letters that felt... different. Like she'd found something in prison that she'd lost years ago. Some piece of herself that I remember from when we were kids." She laughed, but the sound held no joy. "I know how that sounds."

"Like manipulation," I said flatly. "I visited her during the Christmas case, Sophie. She was the same person who tried to kill me in my living room – just with a different hairstyle and a prison uniform."

"You don't understand," Sophie insisted, leaning forward. Her hands gripped the cell bars, knuckles whitening. "I drove to see her two weeks ago. She was... different. Remorseful." Her voice caught slightly. "I thought maybe..."

"Maybe what? She deserved a second chance?" The fluorescent light buzzed like it was offering commentary. "After everything she did?"

"She's still my sister," Sophie said quietly, releasing the bars. She retreated back to her cot, the thin mattress creaking under her weight. "I thought – foolishly, apparently – that maybe she shouldn't have to pay forever." She smoothed her flour-dusted skirt with mechanical precision. "So I contacted Elijah."

"Elijah?"

"Elijah Phillips. We went to high school together – he was two years ahead of me. He's a lawyer now." A small smile touched her lips. "The mysterious man in the suit everyone's been gossiping about."

Understanding dawned like a particularly slow sunrise. "You were looking into reducing her sentence."

Sophie nodded, studying her shoes with intense focus. "At first, I just caught up with him. Texts, calls. Normal things. We met a few times to discuss local legal matters – he helped me with some supplier contracts. But I didn't mention Maggie." Her smile faded. "But yesterday... He drove up – doesn't live far from here. I finally brought up the topic."

"I'm guessing from what Brenda and Mrs. Abernathy observed, it didn't go well."

"That's putting it mildly." Sophie's laugh held an edge sharper than her best bread knife. "He said Maggie's a lost cause. Best case scenario? Twenty-five years before she's eligible for parole, assuming perfect behavior." Her hands returned to twisting in her lap. "We argued. Rather loudly, apparently."

"It was foolish," I said quietly, watching how the cell's shadows seemed to deepen in the growing evening. "Even thinking about her release."

"She's my sister," Sophie repeated, as if those three words could explain everything from murder to manipulations. The cell's lone lightbulb flickered again, creating shifting patterns on the institutional green walls.

The evening silence settled around us, broken only by distant sounds from the front office – Miller presumably losing another game of solitaire while complaining about proper donut storage techniques to an increasingly disinterested night shift.

"Assuming I believe you," I said finally, "I need something concrete to work with. Give me a lead that isn't about family loyalty or prison rehabilitation."

Sophie straightened on her cot, some of her usual energy returning. Her eyes sparked with the same determination I'd seen when she'd first taken over the bakery. "Actually, I might have something. During my interview with Miller, I insisted on seeing that receipt they found. The one with my name on it?"

I nodded, remembering Miller's smug satisfaction.

"Two problems with it," she continued, warming to her topic like she was explaining a particularly complex recipe. "First, my name was printed in all capitals – odd for a receipt. And there were no card digits shown – usually receipts have the last four numbers. But more importantly?" She leaned forward, lowering her voice. "The time stamp shows I was supposedly buying laxatives in Rocky Point at almost exactly the same moment I was purchasing dough at Anderson's here in town."

"You're certain about the time?"

"Absolutely. Nora Anderson asked me for the time since she'd forgotten her phone at home. The receipt's still in my office, showing the time of purchase and the last four digits of my card." Her voice took on an edge of frustration. "And Rocky Point is thirty miles away. Even Miller can't argue I was in two places at once, though he'd probably try if it meant less paperwork."

"Did you tell him this?"

Sophie's expression suggested Miller's response had been less than enthusiastic. "He said he'd 'look into it.' Which in Miller-speak means he filed it under 'Things to Ignore Until They Go Away,' right next to the Christmas tree incident paperwork and that mystery of who keeps stealing his favorite maple bars."

She paused, then added more quietly, "The receipt's still in my office, bottom right drawer of my desk. Along with Maggie's letters, if you want proof I'm telling the truth about those too. I always keep the important papers there."

"The bakery's sealed," I reminded her. Through the small window, I could see the snow falling more heavily now, adding another layer of white to the winter night.

A small smile touched her lips, reminding me briefly of her sister. "Miller probably has some rookie standing guard. And there's a spare key hidden near the back door – under the loose brick three up from the bottom, left side. Been there since before I took over."

"Are you asking me to break into a crime scene?"

"I'm asking you to help prove my innocence," she corrected, her voice carrying the particular determination of someone who's decided truth matters more than legality. "Besides, I called Elijah after my interview with Miller. He's coming tomorrow morning – with that receipt showing I was here in town, he thinks he can at least get me under house arrest while this gets sorted out."

"Time's up, Butterfield!" Miller's voice carried through the door, accompanied by the sound of his computer shutting down and what might have been a frustrated groan at another lost solitaire game. "Some of us have homes to go to. And this donut isn't going to eat itself," he added more quietly.

"Wait," I said as Sophie stood. "What was the name of that shop in Rocky Point? The one on the receipt?"

She frowned, pushing a strand of hair behind her ear. "I didn't catch it when Miller showed me. But he left all the evidence on his desk – that transparent file folder he kept guarding like it contained state secrets instead of petty crime reports."

"If you're quick," she added meaningfully, glancing toward the front office where Miller was already rustling through his coat pockets for his car keys.

I found Miller shrugging into his winter coat, his desk already cleared except for that single folder and what appeared to be a strategic reserve of napkins from various donut shops. His keys jangled impatiently as he waited by the desk.

"Oh, before I go," I said casually, approaching his desk while fumbling with my phone, "could you remind me which form I need to fill out for visitor sign-out? Last time I skipped it you threatened to add me to your 'People Who Create Extra Paperwork' list."

"Really, Butterfield? Now?" Miller's mustache twitched with barely contained impatience. A few sugar granules drifted to the floor like edible snow.

"Won't take a second," I assured him, making a show of dropping my pen near the folder. As I bent to retrieve it, I managed to knock over Miller's favorite "World's Okayest Sheriff" mug, sending him scrambling to save his precious coffee.

"For heaven's sake!" he exclaimed, dabbing at the spreading puddle with his napkin collection. While he was distracted, I activated my phone's camera – or tried to. Instead, what sounded like a full gospel choir began emanating from the speaker, followed by wind chimes and what might have been Emma's attempt at yodeling.

"What in God's name..." Miller straightened, coffee forgotten.

"Sorry," I fumbled with the settings, "Emma's been experimenting with meditation soundscapes. She calls this one 'Cosmic Awakening in D Minor.'"

Taking advantage of his distraction, I quickly snapped several photos while appearing to silence the phone. The images would probably be modern art rather than evidence, but they'd have to do.

"Though I think this is actually her 'Planetary Alignment Polka,'" I added as pan flutes joined the chaos. Miller winced as the volume increased mysteriously. "Or maybe her 'Dance of the Ascending Chakras' – the remixed version."

"Just... stop," Miller pleaded, covering his ears as something that sounded suspiciously like bagpipes merged with the cacophony. "Some of us need our hearing for actual police work."

"Almost got it," I assured him, deliberately hitting every wrong button. A conga beat kicked in, followed by what seemed to be a synthesizer interpretation of cosmic energy.

By the time I "finally" managed to silence the phone, Miller looked ready to ban all technology from the building. His expression suggested he'd rather file paperwork than endure another second of Emma's spiritual soundtrack.

"There," I said brightly, pocketing the device before it could betray me further. "Though you really should consider organizing these files better. Maybe by pastry type? Cross-referenced with sugar content?"

Miller just pointed at the door, his mustache still twitching from the musical assault. I noticed he'd forgotten all about the folder in his haste to escape my phone's spiritual awakening.

Sometimes the best investigative technique was simply being more annoying than suspicious.

\*\*\*

The winter night wrapped around me as I left the station, snow still falling in gentle waves that would have delighted Emma's sense of cosmic significance. The street lights created pools of warm illumination, each one marking another step toward what was probably a terrible idea. Breaking into crime scenes hadn't exactly been covered in my librarian training.

The bakery waited ahead, its darkened windows reflecting the falling snow like mirrors into earlier, happier days. Somewhere inside lay proof of Sophie's innocence – or confirmation of her guilt. Either way, I had to know.

"Been a while since I've broken into a crime scene," I muttered to myself, already missing Ginger's sarcastic commentary. This kind of questionably legal investigation always felt more justified with a talking cat as backup.

He would have had something cutting to say about my amateur burglary techniques.

But Ginger was still recovering in his hospital bed, probably dreaming of premium salmon and properly organized evidence. For now, I'd have to handle this alone.

The snow continued falling as I walked toward the bakery, each step taking me closer to either answers or arrest. Possibly both, given my track record with Miller's patience. But Sophie was right about one thing – the truth had to be in there somewhere, waiting to be discovered among recipes and receipts and sisters' secrets.

Time to find it. Preferably before Miller realized I'd photographed evidence using a phone that was currently trying to teach me meditation in Chinese.

# Chapter 9

The evening air carried the mingled scents of perfume, chocolate, and fresh snow as I walked through Oceanview Cove's transformed streets. Valentine's Day had worked its peculiar magic on our small town, turning even the most practical establishments into scenes from romantic postcards. The hardware store's window featured a display of heart-shaped door knockers arranged around power tools. Even the bait and tackle shop had attempted festivity by tying red ribbons around fishing lures.

Couples filled the sidewalks, each absorbed in their own private worlds. Outside the Harbor View Café, an elderly pair shared a slice of pie, their comfortable silence speaking of decades together. The woman adjusted her husband's scarf with the absent-minded tenderness of long practice, while he pretended not to notice but smiled anyway. Near the town square, a young man in a rumpled suit paced nervously beside a restaurant window, a small velvet box visible in his jacket pocket. His reflection practiced what appeared to be proposal speeches while waiting for his date to arrive.

The scenes stirred memories of my own Valentine's Days with Martha – particularly the year I'd attempted to create a romantic dinner from scratch. The evening had ended with the smoke alarm providing background music while Martha laughed herself breathless at my singed eyebrows and wounded dignity. She'd insisted on photographing me beside the cremated remains of what was supposed to be Beef Wellington, claiming it was "for posterity." The picture still lived in my bedside table, my mortified expression preserved alongside her radiant smile. She'd ordered pizza afterward, and we'd eaten it picnic-style on the living room floor, trading stories about our worst cooking disasters until midnight.

"Special delivery for the lady who married a librarian with culinary aspirations," I'd announced, presenting her with slightly scorched chocolate-covered strawberries. "Only minimally carbonized, I assure you."

The memory dissolved as I reached the corner of the building next to Sophie's bakery. The warm nostalgia of reminiscence gave way to the sharper reality of investigation as I pressed against the cold brick wall, assessing the situation. Just as Sophie predicted, Miller had assigned Officer Martinez to guard duty – the same Martinez whose stellar performance during our last case had involved losing control of a protest and nearly getting trampled by enthusiastic environmentalists.

The young officer stood near the bakery's front door, illuminated by streetlights that caught the powdered sugar still dusting his uniform – an occupational hazard of working with Miller, whose donut consumption had probably single-handedly kept several bakeries in business. Martinez shifted from foot to foot, alternating between checking his phone and staring longingly at the coffee shop across the street.

The front door suddenly opened, spilling warm light onto the street. Mayor Thompson emerged, adjusting his tie with the particular dignity of someone attempting to pretend they haven't spent several hours in the bathroom. His suit showed evidence of his extended occupation – wrinkled in places that suggested prolonged sitting, though he'd made valiant attempts to restore order to both fabric and reputation.

"Officer Martinez!" Thompson announced with forced cheerfulness, his voice carrying the particular strain of someone trying to maintain mayoral dignity after an undignified afternoon. "I cannot thank you enough for your understanding of my... situation. Sometimes a man must stay true to his principles, even in challenging circumstances."

Martinez's expression suggested his principles didn't include extended bathroom occupation or questionable handshaking protocols, but he accepted the mayor's extended hand with professional reluctance. His grimace spoke volumes about proper hygiene and the sacrifices required by public service.

"Consider it a gesture of civic cooperation," Thompson continued, either missing or ignoring Martinez's visible discomfort. "Though perhaps next time I'll exercise more restraint at public events. Those heart-shaped éclairs were truly extraordinary, but seven might have been excessive even for someone of my distinguished position."

He patted his stomach with theatrical regret. "Though I have to admit, Sophie's pastry work is exceptional. The way the chocolate coating complemented the cream f illing..." He trailed off, noticing Martinez's increasing distress. The young officer had begun wiping his hand against his uniform with the desperation of someone mentally calculating the distance to the nearest sink.

"Anyway," Thompson cleared his throat, adjusting his tie again. "Your discretion in this matter is appreciated. Not every officer would understand the unique challenges faced by public officials in... delicate situations."

Martinez muttered something that might have been acknowledgment or a prayer for hand sanitizer.

The mayor turned toward my hiding spot, and I retreated down the narrow street, trying to appear casual. The road offered no convenient escape routes – just snow-covered parking meters and empty newspaper boxes bearing headlines about local parking disputes. My attempt at nonchalance probably resembled someone practicing for a particularly awkward runway show while being chased by bees.

"Mr. Butterfield!" Thompson's voice carried through the evening air with mayoral authority. "Is that you skulking about in such a suspicious manner?"

I turned, adopting what I hoped was a natural expression rather than the guilty look of someone planning to break into a crime scene. "Mayor Thompson. Quite an eventful Valentine's Day, wasn't it?"

"Indeed!" He caught up to me, his breath still carrying hints of Sophie's pastries beneath what smelled like an entire pack of breath mints. "I was just expressing my gratitude to young Martinez for his understanding. Had to engage in some delicate negotiations regarding extended facility use. Very sensitive diplomatic situation."

"Diplomatic being the operative word," I murmured, watching a couple hurry past, their romantic evening plans clearly not involving discussions of mayoral bathroom negotiations.

"I did hear quite the commotion during my... extended stay," he continued, fidgeting with his jazz-playing cupid tie. "Though things became rather muffled when Miller started shouting about crime scenes and evidence collection. Did someone actually expire on the premises? That would be terrible for the health department rating."

I explained briefly about the poisonings, watching his face journey through confusion, relief, and finally understanding.

"You mean I wasn't the only one affected?" His shoulders relaxed visibly, sending new wrinkles cascading through his suit. "Thank heavens! I was beginning to worry my digestive system was staging some sort of political coup. Though I suppose being trapped in a bathroom for hours is preferable to some of the alternatives."

He paused, processing the rest of my explanation. The street light caught the remnants of powdered sugar on his lapel, creating a small constellation of evidence. "But surely Sophie couldn't have... Those éclairs were absolutely divine! No one who creates pastries of that caliber could be capable of such nefarious deeds. It would be like Shakespeare writing grocery lists or Da Vinci painting house numbers."

"My thoughts exactly," I agreed, noting how he kept glancing down the street, probably calculating the distance to his own bathroom. "The evidence seems too convenient."

"Ah!" His eyes lit up with understanding that transformed quickly to embarrassment. "So that's why you're out here doing your detective work. I've interrupted your investigation, haven't I? Here you are, pursuing truth and justice, and I'm rambling about bathroom diplomacy!"

"Something like that," I said carefully, watching how he kept shifting his weight in a way that suggested our conversation might need to end sooner rather than later.

"Say no more!" He backed away, nearly tripping over a parking meter that had probably witnessed more graceful exits. "I won't keep you from your sleuthing. My car's just around the corner – assuming I can remember where I parked. Though perhaps next time, I'll show more restraint at public celebrations. Or at least conduct a proper reconnaissance of available facilities beforehand."

I watched him disappear around the corner, his footsteps crunching in the fresh snow with urgent purpose. A distant car door slammed, followed by the sound of an engine starting with unusual haste.

Returning to my observation point, I found Martinez had moved on to more personal investigations. His exploration of his own nasal cavity showed a dedication to thoroughness that his actual police work often lacked. Each discovery seemed to require extensive analysis under the streetlight.

"Perfect timing," I muttered, preparing to make my move toward the back of the bakery. Just then, my phone erupted in what sounded like a combination of whale songs, wind chimes, and possibly a Gregorian chant having an identity crisis. Martinez's head snapped up, his hand freezing mid-exploration like a child caught stealing cookies.

I ducked back behind the corner, fumbling with my technological nemesis. Sarah's name flashed on the screen alongside what appeared to be Emma's latest attempt at creating cosmic ringtones. Something about "aligning cellular vibrations with planetary movements" – though it sounded more like a symphony orchestra falling down stairs.

"Dad?" Sarah's voice carried immediate concern once I managed to answer. "Are you okay? I just read about what happened!"

"Read about it?"

"The Oceanview Cove Gazette's website. There was mass poisoning at Sophie's bakery! It's all over their local news section. They're saying people were dropping like flies, and the mayor barricaded himself in the bathroom for hours. And you were supposed to be at the Valentine's celebration..."

"The Gazette has a website?" I interrupted, momentarily distracted by this technological revelation. "When did that happen? Last time I checked, they still printed everything on that ancient press in the basement. The one that makes the whole building smell like ink and regret."

"Dad! This is serious! I've been trying to call for the past ten minutes – your phone kept going to voicemail with some woman's voice talking about cosmic alignments and proper astrological times for communication."

"Ah, that would be Emma's work," I sighed. "She must have reconfigured my voicemail settings. I've been wondering why people keep asking me about planetary positions when they leave messages."

"You're deflecting," Sarah said, and I could picture her expression – the same one she used to give me when I tried to explain why her goldfish had mysteriously doubled in size after being replaced. "Were you there? The article mentioned multiple casualties and something about international pastry spies. I've been worried sick!"

"Sorry about that – had a bit of an urgent situation myself," I admitted. "Though not as urgent as the mayor's."

"Dad..."

"I'm fine now," I assured her. "Just lost a few pounds in an unconventional way. Though I may never look at heart-shaped pastries the same way again."

"Only you could find humor in being poisoned," Sarah's laugh carried equal parts relief and exasperation. "I swear, ever since you moved to that town... First Maggie tries to kill you, then Everett rigs a Christmas tree to fall on the square, and now mass poisoning at a Valentine's Day celebration?"

"Getting poisoned wasn't exactly in my Valentine's Day plans," I assured her. "Though the timing could have been worse – at least I made it to my office bathroom."

"And Ginger? Please tell me he's okay! The article didn't mention anything about pets being affected."

"He's recovering at the hospital," I said. "The doctors are treating him just like their human patients – they've even put him in the same room as Emma. Though he keeps turning up his nose at the hospital pillows they provided."

"That sounds like Ginger," Sarah chuckled. "Remember how picky he was with those fancy cat treats I sent him last Christmas? You said he wouldn't even give them a second sniff."

"The same cat who I caught eating pizza crusts out of Mrs. Henderson's garbage last week."

"Speaking of Mrs. Henderson – have you seen the comments section on the article? She's posted about fifteen updates about suspicious vans and foreign license plates. Something about an international pastry crime syndicate targeting small coastal towns?"

"She's been telling me about international conspiracies all morning," I said. "Her theories are getting more creative by the hour."

"But Dad, what about Sophie? The article said she's been arrested. They're claiming she followed in Maggie's footsteps, that it runs in the family. But that can't be right... can it?"

"No," I said firmly. "This feels like a setup. Miller's jumping to conclusions again, just like he did with me during the Peter Johnson case."

"That's what I thought too," Sarah said thoughtfully. "You know what this reminds me of? Those mystery novels you used to read to me when I was little. Remember what you always told me? Sometimes the real culprit is hiding in plain sight – the person you know too well to suspect."

Her words triggered something in my memory, but before I could pursue the thought, Martinez's voice carried around the corner: "Hello? Is someone there? This is a restricted area!"

"Have to go," I whispered. "Duty calls."

"Dad, wait – promise me you'll be careful? After everything that's happened in that town... I worry about you, you know."

"I promise," I assured her. "Besides, I have backup coming from the hospital soon. Ginger would never forgive me if I solved this case without him."

"You're investigating, aren't you?" Sarah's tone suggested she already knew the answer. "That's why you're whispering. Are you somewhere you shouldn't be?"

"That depends entirely on your definition of 'shouldn't be,'" I said. "Let's just say I'm pursuing alternative investigative strategies."

"Just... watch yourself, okay? And call me when you find out who did this. Tom and the kids send their love – Emily's been asking when she'll see her Grandpa and his cat."

"Soon," I promised. "Love you, sweetheart."

"Love you too, Dad. Be safe."

I ended the call, checking the corner again. Martinez had returned to his nasal explorations with renewed enthusiasm. Perfect timing to make my move.

I took one step forward, and a familiar voice behind me nearly made me jump out of my skin.

"Missed me, old man?"

# Chapter 10

I spun around so fast I nearly lost my balance on the snowy sidewalk, my feet sliding on a patch of ice hidden beneath the fresh powder. That familiar sardonic voice – impossible, yet unmistakably real. And there sat Ginger, looking entirely too pleased with himself despite his recent brush with poisoning, perched atop a stack of empty milk crates with his usual regal bearing. His orange fur practically glowed under the streetlight, and a few snowflakes had settled on his whiskers like tiny diamonds.

"You're supposed to be in the hospital!" I managed, keeping my voice low to avoid attracting Martinez's attention. "Unconscious. Recovering. Not materializing out of nowhere like some feline apparition."

"And miss all the fun of investigation?" Ginger settled more comfortably on his makeshift throne, arranging his tail with precise dignity. "Really, Jim. After all our cases together, did you honestly think a minor inconvenience like poisoning would keep me confined to that dreadfully understocked medical facility? Their pillow selection alone was grounds for early departure. Besides, your daughter's namesake – that rather attentive nurse Sarah – gave me something quite remarkable. Felt better almost immediately."

"How did you even-"

"Get here? Simple deduction, really. You're remarkably predictable when it comes to investigation locations. Though I must say, your attempt at stealth needs work. I could hear you muttering to yourself from halfway down the street."

I glanced around nervously, but Martinez remained absorbed in his personal explorations, a man on a mission to discover if his finger could actually reach his brain through his nose.

"What happened after I left this morning?" I asked, crouching down beside Ginger's milk crate pedestal. "Last thing I saw, you were doing a rather convincing impression of Sleeping Beauty."

"Minus the kissing requirement for awakening, thankfully," Ginger sniffed. "I did indeed lose consciousness rather dramatically – though with significantly more style than your ungraceful exit to the facilities. Woke up a few hours ago to Emma's unconscious astrological predictions. Did you know Mercury's retrograde position affects feline recovery rates? According to her sleep-talking, anyway."

"Sarah is probably worried sick. You can't just disappear from a hospital..."

"Oh please. I left a note. Well, technically I arranged some of Emma's crystals into a message. Though given her unconscious state, she's probably interpreting it as a sign of impending astrological convergence rather than a simple notification of departure."

"The nurse gave you some kind of feline medication, didn't she?" I sighed, recognizing the slightly manic energy in his movements. His usual fluid grace had an edge of medication-induced enthusiasm. "That's going to wear off soon. You should be back in bed."

"Spare me the medical advice," his tail swished with mild irritation, dislodging a small avalanche of snow from the crate. "I've had hairballs more threatening than that little poisoning incident."

"Fill me in," he demanded, shifting to find a more comfortable position on his milk crate throne. "I assume I've missed quite the dramatic series of events, judging by our young officer's dedicated nasal explorations. Though I did catch the mayor's hasty departure – his expression suggested a man intimately acquainted with every public restroom between here and his house."

I quickly summarized the day's chaos – the mass poisoning, Sophie's arrest, my interviews with Mrs. Abernathy and Brenda, and finally the revelation about Maggie's prison correspondence. I told him about the fake receipt Miller found with Sophie's name and how there was another receipt in her office that could prove she was at Anderson's at the exact same time, making it impossible for her to be in Rocky Point buying those laxatives. Ginger listened intently, his tail marking key points like a conductor's baton, whiskers twitching at particularly interesting details.

"So our esteemed Sheriff Miller has once again chosen the path of minimal effort," he observed when I finished. "Though I notice his evidence collection seems remarkably convenient – almost as if someone arranged a trail of bread crumbs. Or in Miller's case, donut crumbs."

"I managed to photograph the receipt Miller found," I said, pulling out my phone to show him. "The fake one that supposedly proves Sophie bought those laxatives." The images looked like they'd been taken during an earthquake – mostly blur with occasional glimpses of what might have been text.

"Your ongoing battle with modern technology continues to provide entertainment," Ginger observed, squinting at the screen. "Though I must say, these photos perfectly capture your relationship with digital devices. Is that your thumb in the corner, or an artistic statement about law enforcement inadequacy?"

A sudden clatter from the bakery's direction made us both freeze. Martinez had begun what he probably thought was a stealthy patrol of the front sidewalk, though the effect was somewhat undermined by his continued personal excavation project.

"Sophie mentioned a spare key," I whispered, nodding toward the back of the building. "Hidden under a loose brick. If we can just get past-"

"Oh please," Ginger interrupted, already moving with practiced stealth despite his recent hospital stay. "Amateur burglary hardly presents a challenge. Though your current posture suggests otherwise – you look like someone trying to sneak past a librarian with overdue books."

The back alley offered more shadows than illumination, perfect for questionably legal activities. We crept past dumpsters releasing the particular aroma that suggested someone had forgotten about last week's fish delivery. Stacks of empty boxes created a maze of cardboard and old receipts, telling stories of busy bakery mornings and Sophie's dedication to proper recycling.

"Third brick up on the left," I muttered, running gloved fingers along the cold wall. "Sophie said it would be loose."

The brick moved with surprising ease, revealing a small cavity containing a key that had seen better decades. It left traces of rust on my gloves as I retrieved it, like crumbs of oxidized evidence.

The lock yielded to gentle persuasion, but the door's hinges had other ideas. Their protest echoed through the alley with enough volume to wake not just the dead, but possibly several previous generations.

"Perfect," Ginger muttered as we froze in place. "Why don't you just call Miller directly? Though given your phone skills, you'd probably accidentally order takeout instead."

"At least I'd get the food delivered to the right address," I whispered back. "Unlike someone who once led us three blocks in the wrong direction tracking a suspicious tuna sandwich."

No eager young officer appeared to arrest us. The only sounds were distant traffic, the soft whisper of falling snow, and what might have been Martinez tripping over his own feet somewhere out front.

The bakery's interior felt wrong in darkness – all harsh angles and unfamiliar shadows where warm displays should be. Our footsteps echoed softly despite attempts at stealth, each sound amplified by darkness.

"Signs of chaos," Ginger observed, pausing to study an overturned chair. "Though whether from the poisoning or Miller's enthusiastic evidence collection remains unclear. His technique continues to favor destruction over deduction."

Sophie's office door stood partially open, crime scene tape creating a half-hearted attempt at security. Inside, the small space showed clear signs of Miller's thorough investigation – drawers left askew, papers scattered across the desk like fallen leaves, filing cabinet tilted at an angle that suggested someone had searched it with more enthusiasm than skill. Moonlight filtered through partially closed blinds, creating stripes across the chaos that reminded me uncomfortably of jail cells.

"Check the bottom right drawer," I whispered, remembering Sophie's instructions. "She said Maggie's letters-"

A sudden bang from the front of the bakery made us both jump. Something metal clattered against the tile, followed by Martinez's voice: "Hello? Is anyone there? This is a... um... official police presence!"

"Wonderful," Ginger said dryly. "I don't suppose you've developed an actual plan in the last thirty seconds?"

I fumbled through the drawer, trying to minimize noise while maximizing speed – a combination that resulted in neither. Finally, my fingers found a stack of letters bound with a blue ribbon that had seen better days. The handwriting was unmistakably Maggie's.

"Pure manipulation," I whispered. "All this about finding herself, becoming a better person. Even mentions taking up meditation – though I notice she doesn't specify whether it involves Emma's particular brand of cosmic enlightenment."

"The eternal optimist's burden," Ginger agreed softly. "Though her penmanship remains impressive, even in prison. Unlike your case notes, which continue to resemble a doctor's prescription written during an earthquake."

Martinez's footsteps echoed through the bakery, punctuated by what sounded like him discovering every piece of furniture with his shins. "This is a security check!" he called out, his voice cracking slightly. "I am authorized to use... well, something. Once I remember which pocket has what."

The receipt from Anderson's lay partially buried under a stack of invoices that probably hadn't been urgent even before the poisoning. Its critical timestamp stood out clearly in the dim light. I managed to take a photo without activating any of Emma's meditation apps – a minor miracle in itself. Then, with gloved hands, I carefully retrieved the receipt and tucked it into my coat pocket.

That's when my phone erupted in what could only be described as a gospel choir's enthusiastic interpretation of "Stayin' Alive" – my regular ringtone, not one of Emma's cosmic creations. The sound bounced off the office walls like an announcement of impending arrest.

"Unknown number," I whispered frantically, trying to silence the surprisingly determined choir. "Could be important..."

"Or could be our ticket to shared accommodations with the mayor in his new favorite bathroom," Ginger hissed.

Martinez's footsteps quickened, heading directly toward the office. With no better options, I answered, keeping my voice barely above a breath: "Hello?"

"Mr. Butterfield?" Sarah's voice – the nurse, not my daughter – carried the particular concern of someone who's lost a patient who technically shouldn't have been mobile enough to lose. "I'm sorry to bother you, but we can't find Ginger anywhere. We've checked under every bed, behind every potted plant..."

"He's fine," I whispered, watching Martinez's shadow appear outside the door like a particularly inept harbinger of doom. "He's with me."

"Why are you whispering?" she asked, her voice automatically dropping to match mine. "Is everything okay? You sound like you're hiding in a closet."

"Just a bit busy at the moment," I murmured, watching the doorknob turn with agonizing slowness. "Could we discuss this tomorrow?"

"Of course! But please bring him in for his next dose of medication. He really shouldn't be moving around too much yet."

"First thing tomorrow," I promised quickly. "Have to go!"

I ended the call just as Martinez's flashlight beam cut through the darkness. Ginger and I pressed ourselves against the wall behind the door, barely breathing.

"Hello?" Martinez called out, his voice wavering between authority and uncertainty. "Show yourself! I'm armed!" A pause, then quietly: "Well, probably armed. Just need to remember the security code for this taser..."

He took two hesitant steps into the office. His uniform still bore evidence of Miller's donut proximity – powdered sugar catching the flashlight beam like freshly fallen snow. The light hit a glass paperweight on Sophie's desk, sending rainbow reflections dancing across the walls.

"Oh geez," he muttered, jumping at his own light show. "Nobody said anything about disco ghosts. First the mayor's bathroom saga, now this..." He swallowed audibly. "Get it together, Martinez. Ghost stories are just-"

A sudden gust through the partially open window made the blinds rattle, causing him to release a sound that probably wouldn't make it into his official report.

"Maybe it's just the wind," he assured himself, voice rising an octave. "Or maybe... oh no. What if Miller's donuts were poisoned too? Could be hallucinating. Starting to see things. Hearing things. Having conversations with pastries..."

"His deductive reasoning shows surprising potential," Ginger purred, watching Martinez's continued descent into pastry-based paranoia. "Though his conclusions about Miller's donuts suggest hidden investigative talents."

Martinez began backing toward the door, his flashlight beam now performing what appeared to be an interpretive dance. "Just going to... check the perimeter again," he announced to the empty room. "Nothing suspicious here. Nothing at all. Except maybe ghost pastries. Or donut-induced visions..."

We waited until his retreating footsteps faded, accompanied by what sounded like him discovering every chair in the bakery with his kneecaps. Only then did I release the breath I'd been holding.

"Well," Ginger observed as we crept toward the back door, "that was certainly educational. Though I notice our young officer's grasp of reality seems about as firm as your understanding of smartphone settings."

We made our escape through the back door, carefully returning the key to its brick hiding place. The snow had intensified, transforming the alley into something from a winter fairy tale – though I doubted many fairy tales involved breaking and entering or officers having existential crises over potentially haunted pastries.

"Well," Ginger commented as we walked home through the steadily falling snow, "I must say this ranks among our more creative investigations. Though sneaking past Officer Martinez hardly presents a challenge when he's busy conducting conversations with imaginary pastries."

"At least we got what we came for," I replied. "Though I could have done without the impromptu gospel performance from my phone."

"Your technological mishaps do have impeccable timing," he agreed dryly. "Though Martinez seemed more concerned about haunted donuts than actual intruders."

The streets had emptied as evening deepened. Through restaurant windows, we caught glimpses of couples celebrating Valentine's Day properly – with candlelight and conversation rather than poisonings and amateur burglary.

"We have a busy day tomorrow," I said, noticing how Ginger's pace had slowed slightly. The medication was clearly wearing off. "First stop is getting you back to the hospital for that next dose."

"Absolutely not," he protested, though with less vigor than usual. "I've seen enough of their substandard accommodations."

"Then I suppose you'll have to sit out our trip to Rocky Point," I said casually. "Can't have you passing out while we investigate that suspicious receipt."

He was quiet for several steps, considering. Finally, he sighed with theatrical resignation. "Fine. But only because that nurse Sarah has excellent taste in cream selection."

Movement near the bakery caught my eye. Martinez emerged from the front door, locking up with the exaggerated care of someone who's recently questioned their grip on reality. But something else drew my attention – a shadow, darker than the rest, peering around the corner of the building. I blinked, and it vanished, leaving only swirling snow where it had been.

"Did you see-" I started to ask, but stopped. Probably just imagination, fueled by a long day of investigation and questionably legal activities.

Still, as we walked home through the snowy evening, I couldn't shake the feeling that we weren't the only ones interested in Sophie's bakery tonight. The shadow lingered in my mind, suggesting this case might have more layers than even Miller's rush to judgment had suggested.

But those were questions for tomorrow. For now, the snow continued falling, adding another blanket of white to an already complicated Valentine's Day.

# Chapter 11

Early morning light filtered through the blinds as a cardinal watched from his perch on the maple branch, judging my sleeping habits with his beady stare. My phone's alarm chimed its usual wake-up call – mercifully free of Emma's cosmic additions for once, though I noticed three missed notifications about optimal planetary alignments for morning routines.

I reached over to silence it, already bracing for Ginger's customary sarcastic commentary about my morning coordination or the state of my hair, which probably resembled a bird's nest after a particularly enthusiastic hurricane.

But no witty remarks came. No observations about my bedhead or fumbling attempts to locate the snooze button. Not even a comment about my choice of pajamas, which Martha had given me as a joke – they featured tiny books arranged in proper Dewey Decimal order.

Ginger lay curled on his windowsill perch, still fast asleep. His orange fur caught the morning light, rising and falling with each steady breath. One paw twitched occasionally, suggesting dreams of chasing suspicious characters or critiquing inferior salmon. It was the first time in our months together that I'd woken before him. Usually he was already alert and ready with pointed observations before my eyes even opened.

The medication from yesterday had clearly worn off, leaving him in need of proper rest. Even the sharp knock at my front door failed to rouse him from his slumber – a sound that normally had him analyzing visitor patterns and predicting their intentions before they finished knocking.

I pulled on my robe, mentally calculating the odds of it matching given that I'd dressed in pre-coffee darkness. Through the door's decorative window, I could make out a man in an expensive suit standing on my front porch, his posture suggesting both importance and impatience. Behind him, a sleek black BMW that probably cost more than my house gleamed in the morning sun, its German engineering practically radiating superiority over my aging Buick.

Sophie's lawyer, I realized. She must have been quite optimistic about my burglary skills to send him first thing in the morning. Though given Martinez's ghostly pastry crisis last night, perhaps her confidence wasn't entirely misplaced.

I opened the door to find myself face to face with the mysterious suit-wearing visitor from Sophie's bakery. Up close, his tailoring was even more impressive – the kind of bespoke craftsmanship that made my own wardrobe look like it came from a discount bin at a thrift store. His leather briefcase alone probably cost more than my entire closet, and the watch peeking from his sleeve could likely pay off my car.

"Mr. Butterfield?" He extended a manicured hand. "Elijah Phillips. Sophie mentioned you might have something for me?" His tone carried the particular confidence of someone used to getting exactly what they want, precisely when they want it.

His grip was firm but not aggressive, the handshake of someone who'd perfected the art of professional cordiality. A faint trace of expensive cologne lingered in the air between us, making my own discount drugstore soap feel suddenly inadequate.

"Right," I said, noting how his eyes had already begun scanning my decidedly less polished appearance. "Would you like to come in for coffee? Tea?"

"Thank you, but I really should get Sophie out of that cell." A flash of genuine concern crossed his perfectly composed features, suggesting that despite his polished exterior, he actually cared about more than just billable hours. "She's already spent one night in there – far too long for an innocent woman."

Through the still-open door, a gust of winter air carried the sounds of early morning – birds declaring territorial disputes, a neighbor scraping ice from their windshield with more enthusiasm than skill, the distant rumble of the harbor coming to life.

"Let me get what you need."

My coat still hung by the door where I'd left it after last night's breaking and entering adventure. The receipt felt like it was burning a hole in the pocket – evidence obtained through questionably legal means that could help prove Sophie's innocence. Though explaining its acquisition might require some creative interpretation of investigative techniques.

I retrieved it carefully with gloved hands, not wanting to add any more fingerprints to complicate matters. Elijah studied it intently before sliding it into an evidence bag with practiced precision, his movements suggesting years of handling delicate documents.

"Sophie was right about the timing," he said, sealing the bag with methodical care. "This should be enough to at least get her under house arrest while we investigate further." He tucked the evidence into his briefcase, the soft leather creaking in a way that probably cost extra.

"I hope so," I replied. "Though I should warn you about our local law enforcement's unique approach to investigation. Sheriff Miller's dedication to avoiding paperwork tends to override actual evidence. His filing system is based primarily on donut proximity."

A slight smile touched Elijah's lips. "So I've heard. Sophie filled me in on his particular brand of police work." He reached into his suit jacket, producing a business card. "If you discover anything else relevant to the case, please call me directly."

I accepted the card, noting the understated yet expensive texture. Even his contact information exuded professionalism, though I noticed he'd omitted his hourly rate – probably to avoid causing cardiac events in potential clients.

"I'm heading to Rocky Point today," I said. "Going to look into that store that supposedly issued the fake receipt." A passing mail truck's brakes squealed in protest, as if commenting on my investigative plans.

"Excellent. Keep me posted on what you find." He checked his watch. "I should go start the process of freeing Sophie. Thank you for your help, Mr. Butterfield."

I watched him walk to his car. The vehicle purred to life with the particular sound of German engineering meeting unlimited budget. They disappeared down the street, leaving only a lingering trace of expensive cologne and the weight of his business card in my pocket.

Back inside, Ginger still hadn't stirred from his windowsill sanctuary. The morning sun had crept higher, warming his orange fur. A small puddle of drool suggested his dreams involved premium seafood – a detail I'd be sure to mention later when he inevitably critiqued my morning appearance.

I started the coffee maker and began preparing breakfast, its familiar routine feeling somewhat surreal after the events of the past twenty-four hours. The kitchen filled with the comforting aroma of dark roast, mixed with the particular scent of winter morning seeping through window frames.

The sound of a tuna can opening acted like a magical summoning spell. Suddenly Ginger materialized in the kitchen, all traces of sleep vanishing at the prospect of premium fish. He arranged himself by his food bowl with the particular dignity of someone pretending they hadn't just sprinted at Olympic speeds for canned seafood.

"Ah, Sleeping Beauty finally awakens," I said, watching him settle into his usual breakfast spot. "I was beginning to think I'd need to find a handsome prince. Though given your standards, we'd probably need royalty with premium salmon-catching credentials."

"Everything happens for the first time," he replied, eyeing the tuna with barely concealed interest. "Even me sleeping later than you. Though I notice your morning appearance suggests you could still benefit from several more hours of unconsciousness. That robe in particular appears to be staging some sort of textile rebellion."

I set his breakfast before him, noting how he tried to maintain an air of casual indifference despite his obvious enthusiasm for the tuna. A few snowflakes drifted past the window, as if nature was trying to add garnish to his morning meal. "Such gratitude. And here I thought near-death experiences were supposed to make one more appreciative of life's simple pleasures."

"Near-death is a bit dramatic," he observed between delicate bites. "Though I suppose your tendency toward exaggeration explains those case notes of yours. Next you'll be claiming we faced international pastry assassins coordinating with Martinez's ghost pastries."

The coffee maker finished its morning performance with a final dramatic gurgle. I poured myself a cup, the steam rising in patterns that Emma would probably interpret as cosmic messages. A neighbor's cat wandered past our window, paused to judge our morning routine, then continued on its way with typical feline disdain.

"Speaking of which," I said, settling at the table with my coffee, "we need to visit the hospital for your next dose. Then on to Rocky Point."

This time he didn't protest, though his tail twitched slightly at the mention of returning to medical care. "I suppose proper investigation requires one to be fully functional. Though their pillow selection remains criminally inadequate. Even Miller would be forced to file paperwork about that level of negligence."

***

The morning traffic was lighter than usual as we drove to the hospital. The previous day's chaos had apparently convinced many locals to stay home, probably nursing their own Valentine's Day aftermath. Even Mrs. Henderson's usual morning surveillance post on her front porch sat empty, though her curtains twitched suspiciously as we passed.

The hospital parking lot showed signs of improvement – fewer emergency vehicles, more orderly arrangement of cars suggesting things had calmed considerably. A seagull perched atop a "No Parking" sign, critiquing my parking technique with harsh commentary.

Inside, the halls carried a sense of returning normalcy. The overwhelming scent of antiseptic remained, but the frantic energy of yesterday had been replaced by routine efficiency. A few patients still occupied waiting room chairs, though they looked more inconvenienced than distressed.

Sarah met us near the nurses' station, her teddy bear scrubs somehow managing to look both professional and welcoming. The bears appeared to be having a picnic across her pockets, complete with tiny honey pots.

"There's my escape artist!" she said, reaching for Ginger. "You had me worried sick, young man."

"Young man?" Ginger muttered as she scooped him up. "I'm probably older than her in cat years. Though I notice her technique with proper feline handling suggests hidden talents. Unlike that intern yesterday who apparently learned animal care from wrestling videos."

Sarah turned to me, concern crossing her features. "How are you feeling? You were poisoned too, after all."

"Much better," I assured her. "Nothing some quality time with indoor plumbing couldn't fix."

Sarah nodded, adjusting her grip on a distinctly disgruntled Ginger. "Good. And did you succeed with your secret mission last night?" Her eyes sparkled with curiosity that reminded me powerfully of my daughter. "I figured you must have been up to something important, given all that whispering."

"Something like that," I said, watching how she cradled Ginger with practiced care despite his attempts to maintain dignity. His expression suggested he was mentally cataloging every violation of proper feline transport protocols. "Let's just say it was a productive evening."

She nodded knowingly. "Well, I hope you find who did this. Yesterday was pure chaos – though everyone pulled together brilliantly." Her expression turned apologetic. "We had to give Emma a new roommate since this troublemaker left. Another Valentine's Day casualty."

"How dare they," Ginger muttered, though his indignation seemed somewhat undermined by how comfortably he was settled in Sarah's arms. "My precisely arranged pillows, commandeered by some interloper. I suspect Emma's crystals failed to protect my territorial claims."

"I'll take him for his medication," Sarah said. "Why don't you visit Emma? Mr. O'Connell is already there."

Emma's room felt different without Ginger's presence. The space had been divided by a privacy curtain, beyond which someone was producing impressive snoring sounds that seemed to vibrate the very walls. The noise had a particular rhythm to it, like a jazz musician attempting to play a trombone underwater.

Emma lay peaceful in her bed, still unconscious but occasionally muttering about planetary alignments and cosmic convergences. Her constellation dress continued its gentle twinkling despite its owner's state, creating tiny light shows on the ceiling. "Neptune suggests caution when approaching pastries in retrograde," she murmured, her hands moving as if arranging invisible crystals.

Shawn sat beside her, looking remarkably alert for the early hour. His usual bartender's apron had been replaced by casual clothes, though he still carried himself with the particular awareness of someone used to monitoring rowdy customers. A takeout coffee cup from Rose's sat beside him, suggesting he'd already made his morning rounds.

"Morning," he greeted me quietly. "Quite the symphony we've got going here." He nodded toward the curtain. "Chuck's been providing the percussion section since they brought him in."

"Chuck?" I asked, gesturing toward the curtain, where another particularly impressive snore suggested someone was attempting to communicate with distant galaxies.

Shawn nodded, absently adjusting Emma's blanket. "Chuck managed to get a double dose. First, the laxative got him – spent a good hour in the bathroom. Then, still hungry and apparently lacking any sense of self-preservation, he pulled out one of those Valentine's treats he'd pocketed earlier. Figured the laxative couldn't hit him twice." Shawn shook his head. "Ten minutes later, he was unconscious in the hallway. They figured Ginger's bed was free, so..."

"Have you been here all night?" I asked, settling into the chair beside him.

"Nah, just got here about ten minutes ago," he replied. "Bar was dead last night – turns out mass poisoning isn't great for business. Who knew?" His attempt at humor couldn't quite mask the concern in his eyes. "Went to bed early, figured I should stop by to check on Emma."

Through the window, morning sunlight created patterns across Emma's constellation dress, making it seem like the stars were still twinkling faintly despite their owner's unconscious state. Her crystals had been carefully arranged on the bedside table, probably by Shawn's attentive hands, though several appeared to have rolled into positions that would probably horrify her sense of cosmic alignment.

"Mars suggests caution when realigning serving trays," Emma muttered, her hands moving as if mixing invisible drinks. "The stars are particularly sensitive to proper garnish placement."

"How's our feline investigator?" Shawn asked, his voice nearly drowned out by Chuck's impressive snoring symphony.

I filled him in on our evening adventure – the breaking and entering, Martinez's ghost pastry crisis, and our plans for Rocky Point. His expression shifted between amusement and concern as I described Ginger's medication-fueled assistance.

"So Martinez thought the bakery was haunted by vengeful pastries?" Shawn chuckled. "Though given some of Maggie's old recipes, that might not be too far off."

"Wish I could join you," Shawn said as another snore rattled the window panes. "But I should stay here, wait for Emma to wake up. Maybe she'll remember something important about yesterday morning at the bakery. Though at this rate, Chuck's snoring might keep her in a cosmic trance indefinitely."

"Venus disapproves of improper soufflé technique," Emma contributed, as if on cue. Her hands traced mysterious patterns in the air.

"Where's Robert?" I asked, noticing the fisherman's absence. An orderly passed by pushing a squeaky cart, its wheels providing an odd counterpoint to Chuck's nasal symphony.

"Got a big order he couldn't postpone. He's out at sea." Shawn replied, adjusting Emma's blanket.

"Any useful gossip at the bar last night?" I asked. "Even with the low turnout, someone must have had theories. Our town's never been short on creative speculation."

Shawn chuckled, though the sound held little humor. "Oh, plenty of theories. Some folks say Sophie finally cracked, decided to follow her sister's footsteps. Others think Mrs. Abernathy orchestrated the whole thing to take over the bakery herself – probably to enforce proper pastry protocol across town."

I laughed at that, but something about the idea nagged at my memory – a connection just out of reach, like trying to remember a dream after waking. Before I could pursue the thought, Sarah appeared with a distinctly disgruntled Ginger in her arms.

"All set," she announced cheerfully, transferring him to my care despite his attempts to restore dignity through strategic squirming. "Just need to come back this afternoon for the final dose."

Ginger immediately jumped to the floor, arranging himself with exaggerated precision. "The indignity of being carried like a common housecat," he muttered, grooming his ruffled fur with intense focus.

"Call if you need anything," Shawn said as we prepared to leave. Through the curtain, Chuck's snoring had taken on an almost musical quality, like a jazz solo performed entirely through nose whistles. "And let me know if you find anything in Rocky Point."

"Same goes for you," I replied. "Especially if Emma wakes up remembering anything useful beyond cosmic pastry predictions."

***

The morning had fully arrived as we walked to my car, sunlight catching the last remnants of yesterday's snow.

The hospital parking lot had filled with regular visitors now, their cars arranged in the particular chaos that seems unique to medical facilities.

"I notice Mrs. Henderson's suspicious minivan theory seems to have infected the entire town," I observed. "That pink minivan is getting some very judgmental looks."

"Probably because its license plate suggests out-of-state origins," Ginger commented as we reached the car. "Though your observation skills regarding suspicious vehicles would benefit from remembering where we actually parked. We've been walking in the wrong direction for the past minute."

He was right. We turned around, retracing our steps past a group of nurses heading home after the night shift. One waved to Ginger, who pretended not to notice while secretly preening.

My car sat exactly where we'd left it, though the seagull had apparently used my windshield for target practice. "Nature's critics are everywhere," Ginger observed as I cleaned the glass. "Though I notice their artistic expression lacks subtlety."

Time to see what Rocky Point could tell us about fake receipts and framed bakers. The pieces were there – we just needed to find out how they fit together.

"Ready for another adventure?" I asked as Ginger settled into his usual spot, arranging himself for optimal travel comfort.

"As long as it doesn't involve more hospital visits or Martinez's pastry-based existential crises," he replied. "Though I must admit, being in Sarah's capable hands was significantly more comfortable than this ancient car seat."

"Still better than being transported in a bar apron," I commented, starting the engine.

Ginger's head snapped up. "What exactly do you mean by that?"

"I'll tell you on the way."

The morning traffic moved steadily as we headed for Rocky Point, carrying us toward whatever answers – or questions – awaited. The town lay ahead, holding its secrets like cards in a poker game. We were about to see what the dealer had in store.

# Chapter 12

"It was either being transported in Shawn's bar apron or laying there unconscious," I explained as we crossed the town line into Rocky Point.

"I maintain that the entire situation was beneath my dignity," Ginger replied, still grooming imaginary bar apron residue from his fur. He'd spent the entire thirty-minute drive alternating between complaining about being "delivered like a bar snack" (exactly as I'd predicted) and detailing the numerous violations of proper feline transport protocols. "The fabric wasn't even Egyptian cotton. And it probably smelled distinctly of last week's wing special. With notes of ranch dressing that I suspect will never fully leave my fur."

The Rocky Point welcome sign appeared ahead, its faded paint suggesting the town's maintenance budget focused on more pressing matters than first impressions. A seagull perched atop it, adding its own artistic contribution to the weathered surface while judging our arrival with beady-eyed suspicion.

"Now we just have to find this store," I said, pulling into a small strip mall parking lot. The asphalt bore the particular patchwork quality of multiple repair attempts, each one seemingly less successful than the last. A shopping cart with a rebellious wheel performed lazy circles in the breeze, like a drunken ballet dancer refusing to leave the stage.

I pulled out my phone, already dreading the technological battle ahead. "The GPS should be able to-"

"Here we go again," Ginger sighed, settling more comfortably into his seat.

The app took several attempts to open, each failure accompanied by increasingly creative error messages that suggested my phone had developed both a personality disorder and a questionable sense of humor. When it finally loaded, the blue dot representing our location appeared to think we were somewhere in Manitoba.

"That can't be right," I muttered, turning the phone different angles as if that might help convince it we weren't in Canada. "Unless we took a very wrong turn at that last light and somehow crossed an international border without noticing."

"Your grasp of geography rivals Miller's understanding of proper evidence storage," Ginger observed dryly. "Though I must say, Canada might be an improvement over your usual navigational achievements."

We spent the next twenty minutes following the GPS's increasingly questionable directions through Rocky Point's maze-like streets. Each "recalculating" brought us to another dead end or parking lot, while my phone's cheerful voice suggested turns that would have required either a helicopter or the ability to drive through buildings. At one point, we found ourselves in the loading dock of a seafood restaurant, where a chef on his smoke break watched us execute a seventeen-point turn with the kind of fascinated horror usually reserved for watching train wrecks.

"You've arrived at your destination," the phone announced triumphantly as we faced our third brick wall of the morning.

"Unless our store has recently converted to selling bricks wholesale, I suspect your technological companion might be slightly confused," Ginger observed, watching a pigeon inspect our latest dead end with more interest than it deserved. "Though this wall does have a certain retail charm. Perhaps it's having a sale on mortar."

After our fifth attempt ended at what appeared to be someone's backyard chicken coop – complete with very judgmental hens who seemed personally offended by our intrusion – I finally admitted defeat. "This isn't working."

"Your powers of deduction continue to astound," Ginger commented as we pulled up to a stoplight. "Though I notice the chickens seemed more directionally aware than your phone. Perhaps we should have asked them for directions. They certainly couldn't do worse than your technological tour of local poultry establishments."

An elderly woman crossed in front of us, her shopping bags suggesting intimate knowledge of local retail locations. Her hat featured what appeared to be artificial fruit arranged with more enthusiasm than artistic merit.

"Excuse me," I called out, rolling down my window. "Could you tell me where Ready Mart is? The convenience store?"

"Oh, Ralph's place?" She shifted her bags, one of which appeared to be leaking something mysterious onto the sidewalk. "Two blocks that way, can't miss it. Red brick building, usually has a cat sleeping in the window. Though that cat's been there so long, some of us suspect it might be stuffed." She peered at my car more closely, her hat's artificial cherries bobbing dangerously. "You're practically there already. Been driving around a while?"

"Only long enough to tour every chicken coop in Rocky Point," I replied with a self-deprecating smile. "Thank you for the directions."

Ready Mart occupied a corner slot in a modest strip mall, sandwiched between a laundromat and what appeared to be the world's most depressing tax preparation office. True to the woman's word, an ancient orange tabby dozed in the front window, its impressive girth suggesting it had been sampling the store's wares rather liberally. A neon "OPEN" sign flickered with the particular inconsistency of something that had given up caring about proper illumination years ago.

The store's interior carried that unique scent of beef jerky, coffee that had been sitting too long, and whatever mysterious combination of chemicals created "new car scent" air fresheners. Fluorescent lights buzzed overhead in a way that suggested they were plotting rebellion.

A radio behind the counter played soft rock hits from the 90s, though the speaker's quality made every song sound like it was being performed underwater. In the corner, a slush machine that had seen better decades gurgled ominously.

We walked the aisles first, observing without being obvious about it. The store followed the usual convenience layout – snacks, drinks, questionable hot dogs rotating endlessly on their metal rollers, and a small medication section tucked in the back corner as if embarrassed by its presence.

The laxative in question sat innocently on its shelf between antacids and something promising 24-hour relief from an ailment I'd rather not contemplate. I found myself staring at it, as if it might spontaneously confess to its role in our Valentine's Day disaster.

"I realize you're having a moment with the laxative," Ginger commented, "but perhaps we should focus on actual investigation rather than antagonizing pharmaceutical products."

At the counter, a young woman in her early twenties stood arranging candy bars with the particular determination of someone who'd been told to "look busy" during slow periods. Her name tag declared her to be "Jenny," though someone had added a small heart over the 'y' in what appeared to be pink nail polish. Her uniform vest had seen better days, but she'd attempted to brighten it with an assortment of pins featuring cats in various states of sass. One declared "Purr-fessional Cat Lady in Training," while another showed a cat knocking a coffee mug off a table with the caption "Gravity Testing in Progress."

"Can I help you?" she asked, abandoning a particularly stubborn Snickers bar to its misaligned fate.

"Actually, yes," I said, noting how her fingers kept drifting back toward the uncooperative candy display. "Two days ago, at 2:15 PM, someone purchased this specific laxative here." I gestured toward the shelf where I'd been having my staring contest with pharmaceutical products. "Any chance you remember who bought it?"

Jenny's face scrunched in thought, her cat pins catching the fluorescent light. One pin featuring a grumpy-looking Siamese seemed to be judging my investigative technique. "Sorry, that wasn't my shift. I just started last month – only work mornings and weekends. Trying to save up for vet tech school," she added with the particular hopefulness of someone still believing in career dreams.

"Who was working then?"

"That would've been Owen's shift," she said, finally surrendering to temptation and adjusting the Snickers bar. "But he took the whole week off right after that shift. Kind of weird timing, actually. Left me with all these extra hours to cover."

"Took the week off?" I repeated, catching Ginger's slight tail twitch that suggested he'd noticed the same oddity. "Right after that shift specifically?"

Ginger's attention had fixed on something above the counter – a security camera aimed directly at the register, its red light blinking with steady purpose like a tiny electronic conscience. He cleared his throat meaningfully, the sound carrying clear meaning to me if not to Jenny: We can't wait a week for Owen to return.

"Would it be possible to review the security footage from that time?" I asked, watching how Jenny's hands immediately started twisting her vest hem, nearly dislodging a pin that declared "Cats are like potato chips... you can't have just one!"

"Oh, I don't know..." she hesitated, glancing toward what appeared to be a manager's office, its frosted glass window suggesting either important business dealings or an excellent napping spot. "We're not really supposed to show that to strangers. I mean, I just started here, and I really need this job, and my cat needs dental surgery..."

For the first time since Sarah had sent it as a joke gift, I reached for the private investigator badge clipped to my belt. In Oceanview Cove, everyone knew me – badge or not, I could investigate almost anywhere. But here in Rocky Point, I was just another stranger asking suspicious questions about laxatives, which admittedly did sound rather questionable.

I opened my coat slightly, letting the badge catch the light. "I'm a private investigator," I said, trying to sound more authoritative than I felt. "Currently investigating a murder case in Oceanview Cove. This footage could be crucial evidence."

Ginger's whiskers twitched with barely contained amusement at my attempt at official-sounding dialogue, but Jenny's eyes widened at the word "murder." The slush machine chose that moment to emit a particularly ominous gurgle, as if providing sound effects for dramatic revelations.

"Oh! I... I guess that's different then," she said, already moving toward the computer behind the counter, nearly knocking over a display of energy drinks in her haste. "Just... please don't tell Ralph I showed you. I really can't afford to lose this job. My cat's already judging me for the generic brand food."

Her fingers moved across the keyboard with the particular uncertainty of someone still learning a new system. After several false starts and what appeared to be an accidental activation of the store's loudspeaker system (treating us all to a burst of static and half a morning announcement about two-for-one beef jerky), she finally pulled up the security footage.

"That's... weird," she said, frowning at the screen while absently straightening her "Cats Against Monday Mornings" pin.

"What's weird?"

"There's like, ten minutes missing. Right around that time you mentioned." She turned the monitor slightly so I could see. "See? Here's Owen eating his lunch, then it jumps ahead ten minutes, and suddenly he's typing something on the computer."

I moved behind the counter for a better view, carefully navigating around a cardboard display of energy shots that looked ready to collapse if someone breathed too hard. Sure enough, the footage showed Owen – a man in his thirties whose abundance of tattoos and spiked hair suggested he moonlighted in a punk band that hadn't quite made it – consuming what appeared to be a microwave burrito with the enthusiasm of someone who'd lost their sense of taste years ago. Then the timestamp jumped exactly ten minutes, revealing him at the register looking slightly more alert but also slightly green around the edges.

"Any chance you could tell me where Owen lives?" I asked, watching Jenny's expression shift back to uncertainty faster than the hot dogs rotated on their eternal journey.

"Oh, I really shouldn't... that's kind of confidential employee information..." Her hands found another pin to fidget with, this one declaring "Pawsitively Exhausted."

I adjusted my coat again, letting the badge peek out meaningfully. Jenny's resistance crumbled faster than the store's day-old pastries in the discount bin.

"Here," she said, scribbling an address on the back of a receipt for beef jerky and something called "Extreme Energy Blast." "But you didn't get this from me, okay? I've got four cats to feed."

"Could you tell me how to get there?" I asked quickly, before my GPS could suggest another tour of local poultry establishments. "Preferably without any advanced navigation technology?"

After receiving surprisingly clear directions that involved actual street names rather than "recalculating," I remembered one final detail. "Quick question – do your receipts normally show customer names?"

"Um, not sure actually," Jenny admitted, straightening her vest pins nervously. A small collection of cat hair drifted from the fabric, suggesting her "Crazy Cat Lady" pin wasn't just aspirational. "They mentioned something about it in training, maybe some setting in the register app for card payments? I was kind of distracted because there was a stray cat in the parking lot that day..."

"Only one way to find out," I said, reaching for a bottle of iced coffee from the nearby cooler.

"Iced coffee? Really?" Ginger commented from his observation post near the candy display. "Your beverage choices continue to disappoint. Though I must say, your badge presentation was quite effective. Only minimal fumbling and just a slight squeak when you said 'crucial evidence.' Almost professional, in a small-town amateur detective sort of way."

The coffee's price tag suggested either inflation had reached new heights or convenience stores had developed delusions of premium beverage grandeur. I presented my credit card to Jenny, who processed the transaction with the careful concentration of someone still memorizing register procedures while simultaneously trying not to think about cat food prices.

The receipt she handed me confirmed our suspicions – no customer name, just the last four digits of my card number and evidence that I'd drastically overpaid for mediocre coffee.

"Thank you," I said, pocketing both the receipt and my questionably chosen beverage. "You've been incredibly helpful."

Back in the car, Ginger settled into his seat with his usual precise arrangement of limbs. The fat orange tabby in the window had finally opened one eye to acknowledge our departure, though its expression suggested we hadn't earned its full attention.

"Well," Ginger said as I started the engine, "it seems our friend Owen has some explaining to do."

"Ten minutes of missing footage," I mused, following Jenny's directions toward Owen's address. "Exactly when that fake receipt was supposedly issued."

"Indeed," Ginger agreed. "And conveniently timed vacation right after. Our punk rock friend seems to have interesting ideas about surveillance footage maintenance."

Owen's explanation would need to be remarkably good to explain both the missing footage and his convenient vacation timing. Though given recent events in our small town, I had a feeling his story might add yet another layer to our already complicated Valentine's Day mystery.

"He'd better have one hell of an explanation," I said, turning onto the street that would lead us to Owen's house.

"Preferably one that doesn't involve ghost pastries," Ginger added, watching the houses pass by.

The late morning sun slanted across the town, transforming Rocky Point's modest streets into something almost picturesque. Somewhere ahead lay answers – or at least better questions. Soon we'd find out which Owen would provide.

# Chapter 13

The late morning sun painted the quiet street in shades of pale winter gold as we pulled up to the curb. Owen's house huddled at the end of the row, a misfit among its well-maintained neighbors, like that one musician who shows up to a black-tie event in ripped jeans and a vintage band t-shirt. Where other homes boasted fresh paint and manicured lawns, Owen's place seemed determined to single-handedly redefine Rocky Point's property values.

The small ranch-style dwelling had the particular shabbiness of a place whose owner considered home maintenance somewhere between optional hobby and mild annoyance. Paint peeled from the siding in artistic patterns that suggested either modern art or aggressive neglect. The front steps had developed a concerning tilt that made them look more like a skate ramp than actual stairs.

The yard contained an eclectic collection of what might have been art installations or forgotten projects – motorcycle parts arranged in vaguely sculptural formations, hubcaps catching sunlight like budget disco balls. Wind chimes crafted from old guitar strings and what appeared to be broken drumsticks created discordant music in the winter breeze, their tetanus-inducing edges glinting dully.

A rusted basketball hoop hung above the garage at an angle that suggested either modern art or impending collapse. Its net had long since disintegrated, leaving only a few threads that waved in the breeze like surrender flags.

"I see our friend's dedication to alternative aesthetics extends beyond personal appearance," Ginger observed as I navigated around a suspiciously dark patch of ice. "That mailbox appears to be having an existential crisis."

He wasn't wrong – the mailbox listed so dramatically it seemed to be auditioning for a role in a disaster movie. The numbers had faded into vague suggestions rather than actual digits, like an abstract artist's interpretation of what numbers might look like in a parallel universe.

A plastic flamingo stood guard near the front walk, though someone had spray-painted it black and given it tiny skull stickers for eyes. It regarded us with the particular judgment only a goth lawn ornament can achieve.

Movement caught my attention – Owen emerged from his garage, pulling the door closed behind him. Through the briefly open doorway, I caught a glimpse of metallic pink paint that sparked something in my memory, but before I could focus on it, Owen moved to block my view like a bouncer at an exclusive club.

In person, Owen's appearance made the security footage look like a job interview photo. His hair defied both gravity and conventional color theory, spiked into a mohawk that appeared to have been styled with industrial adhesive and dyed a shade of purple that probably hadn't existed before nuclear power. Multiple piercings caught the weak winter sun, creating a light show that could probably be seen from space.

His tattoos created a chaotic narrative up both arms – dragons chasing Japanese characters that likely meant "chicken nugget special" rather than "eternal wisdom," song lyrics written in a font that sacrificed readability for angst, and what appeared to be his old band's logo featuring a guitar-wielding octopus. His faded t-shirt advertised "Toxic Hamster Revolution: World Domination Tour 2019" though something told me the tour hadn't made it past Rocky Point's town limits.

Combat boots that had seen more mosh pits than actual combat completed his ensemble, their steel toes gleaming dully in the winter sun. A wallet chain long enough to secure the Crown Jewels swung from his belt, creating metallic music with each movement.

As I stepped from the car, his eyes locked onto mine with an intensity that suggested recognition. Fear flickered across his features before being masked by what he probably thought was casual indifference but looked more like someone remembering they'd left their iron plugged in.

"You look like you've seen a ghost," I said, noting how his fingers twitched at my words.

He moved closer, bringing with him an odd chemical smell that seemed out of place – sharp and artificial, like cleaning products but with an underlying note I couldn't quite identify.

"Not used to strangers parking on my sidewalk," he replied, his tone aiming for casual but landing somewhere between suspicious and constipated. "Especially not in cars that look like they remember the Nixon administration."

"Speaking of remembering things," Ginger muttered, "I notice our punk rock friend seems to have developed selective amnesia regarding basic property maintenance. Though his chemical aroma suggests at least a passing acquaintance with cleaning supplies, even if they've never met his front yard."

"Private investigator," I explained, reaching for my badge. Unlike Jenny's wide-eyed response, Owen regarded it with all the enthusiasm of someone being shown a tax audit. If anything, the sight of official credentials seemed to activate his inner rebellious teenager. "From Oceanview Cove. Currently investigating a murder."

A short laugh escaped him, though it carried all the humor of a funeral march. "Think you've got the wrong town, man. This is Rocky Point. Oceanview Cove's that way." He jerked his thumb vaguely eastward, his bangles creating a symphony of metallic clinks. A chain around his neck featured what appeared to be guitar picks from bands that had probably disbanded before their first encore.

"His directional sense rivals your technological prowess," Ginger commented dryly. "Though I notice his assessment of questionable decisions seems rather ironic given what appears to be a tattoo of a breakdancing penguin on his forearm."

"Oh, I'm exactly where I need to be," I assured Owen. "Though perhaps we should continue this discussion inside?"

"I'm good here." He crossed his arms, creating a cacophony of metal that probably served as his personal theme music. "Not big on letting strangers from other towns into my house. Bad for the feng shui, you know?"

"Right," I said, noting how his eyes kept darting toward the garage. "Because nothing disrupts spiritual harmony quite like visitors. Though that chemical smell you're wearing seems to be doing a pretty good job of it already."

His hand moved unconsciously to his shirt, which seemed to confirm my suspicion about the source of the odor. Something about that smell nagged at my memory – sharp, artificial, with undertones that reminded me of something I should recognize.

"Let's cut to the chase," I said, watching how his fingers kept adjusting a studded bracelet. "Two days ago, someone made an interesting purchase at Ready Mart during your shift. Ten packs of laxatives. Ring any bells?"

"Lots of people buy those," he shrugged, though the movement had all the naturalness of a robot attempting casual Friday. "Digestive health's a real concern these days. Could've been anyone."

"Not in those quantities," I countered. "Must have been memorable. Especially since the security footage from that exact time frame seems to have gone missing. One minute you're enjoying what looked like a microwave burrito that probably violated several Geneva Conventions, next thing we see is you typing something on the computer. Quite the coincidence."

His eyes widened slightly before he caught himself, like someone remembering they'd left incriminating evidence in plain sight. A muscle twitched beneath the tattoo of what might have been a phoenix or possibly just a chicken having an identity crisis.

"Could be a malfunction," he said, shifting his weight between boots. "Those cameras are ancient, like everything else in that place." His tone hardened. "Though I'm curious how you got access to that footage."

"Private investigators have our ways," I replied smoothly, watching his reaction.

"If that little punk Jenny let you-" he started, voice rising along with his hair.

"Jenny?" I interrupted, seizing the opportunity. "Don't know any Jenny. Ralph showed me himself. Wonderful man, very cooperative when it comes to investigating murder cases."

Real fear crossed Owen's face at the mention of Ralph's name. The chemical smell grew stronger as he shifted nervously, like a walking advertisement for industrial cleaning products gone wrong.

"Though Ralph wasn't too happy about that missing footage," I added, pressing my advantage. "Said something about 'dealing with it' when you get back from vacation. Speaking of which – bit odd timing for time off, isn't it? Middle of winter, and somehow I doubt you're headed to any beaches. Unless there's a Goth resort I haven't heard about."

"None of your business," he snapped, defensive anger replacing fear. His hand moved to his neck, rubbing at a tattoo that appeared to be Chinese characters – though given the quality, it probably translated to "discount sushi Tuesday" rather than whatever profound statement he'd intended.

"Actually, it is my business," I said, letting the friendly facade drop. "Because right now, the picture isn't looking great for you, Owen. Someone bought laxatives during your shift – laxatives that were used to poison people at a Valentine's Day celebration in Oceanview Cove. That poisoning resulted in at least one death. A receipt for that purchase turned up at the crime scene – a receipt that looks suspiciously fake since your store doesn't normally print customer names. And by amazing coincidence, the security footage from that exact transaction is missing, followed by you suddenly taking a week's vacation."

"That fancy badge make you think you're a real cop?" Owen's voice carried a tremor beneath its attempted bravado. The winter breeze caught his mohawk, making it wave like a purple warning flag. "Because I don't know what you're trying to say, but if you're accusing me of something..."

"Just connecting some interesting dots," I said, studying his reaction. "Like that chemical smell, for instance. Trying to clean something off that pink car in your garage?"

His face paled beneath his piercings. "You can't just come here and-"

My phone's ringtone cut through the tension – mercifully free of Emma's cosmic additions for once. Shawn's name flashed on the screen, accompanied by what appeared to be a new meditation app notification about proper alignment of cellular chakras during Mercury's retrograde.

"Got two pieces of news," he said when I answered. "Good and bad. Which do you want first?"

"Give me the good," I replied, watching Owen pretend to be fascinated by his own tattoos while obviously straining to hear my conversation. His fingers kept moving to his collar, adjusting it with nervous energy.

"Emma's awake," Shawn's voice carried both relief and excitement. "And she remembered some interesting details about yesterday morning. Though she keeps insisting Venus told her through a dream about proper pastry arrangement techniques and something about Neptune's influence on proper napkin folding."

"That's fantastic," I said, already wondering what Emma might have noticed before chaos erupted – and how much of it would involve planetary alignments versus actual evidence.

"And the bad news?"

"Miller found new evidence against Sophie," Shawn replied grimly. "And this time... it looks pretty solid. Though knowing Miller, it's probably filed under 'P' for 'Pastry-Related Crimes' or 'B' for 'Bakery Betrayal.'"

I studied Owen, then glanced at the garage where that mysterious pink car lurked in the shadows. My gut told me he wasn't going anywhere – he had a house here, that fancy car, and if he'd been involved in the poisoning and wanted to run, he would have done it already rather than taking a conspicuous vacation at home. Besides, someone who spent that much time and money on hair dye probably had a favorite stylist nearby. No, Owen would still be here when we needed answers. Right now, Oceanview Cove needed us more.

"We're heading back," I told Shawn. "Be there in thirty minutes, assuming my GPS doesn't try routing us through Canada again."

# Chapter 14

"Maybe you should focus your investigation in Oceanview Cove," Owen called after us as we headed back to the car. "Where all this actually happened."

I turned, fixing him with a steady look. "Oh, I plan to look everywhere the evidence leads. Including that garage of yours." I raised two fingers to my eyes, then pointed them at him in the universal "I'm watching you" gesture.

Owen mimicked the motion with significantly more fingers and considerably less subtlety. The movement caused his wallet chain to create a metallic symphony that probably doubled as his band's percussion section.

"These punks today," Ginger sighed as I slid into the driver's seat. "Not a shred of respect for elder investigators. Though I notice his gesture vocabulary seems remarkably expansive for someone who can't maintain basic lawn care. And that gothic flamingo appears to be judging our departure with more dignity than its owner."

"Probably practiced those moves in front of a mirror," I agreed, starting the engine. "Right after perfecting his 'I'm too punk for yard work' attitude."

The morning sun caught Owen's mohawk as he watched us pull away, the purple spikes creating shadows that looked like some kind of exotic sea creature had taken up residence on his head. His collection of motorcycle parts seemed to wave goodbye in the winter breeze, their rusty edges catching the light like budget disco balls. Through the rearview mirror, I saw him glance nervously toward his garage before disappearing inside it, his combat boots leaving perfect circles in the untended snow.

I pulled Elijah's business card from my pocket, admiring again the subtle texture of the expensive paper. My phone took several attempts to dial, somehow managing to activate what sounded like a Tibetan monastery's greatest hits before I got it right.

"Might want to put it on speaker," Ginger suggested as I juggled phone and steering wheel while navigating around a pothole that looked deep enough to have its own postal code. "Unless you're attempting to recreate Martinez's ghost pastry crisis through vehicular interpretive dance. Though I must say, your current driving style suggests more 'haunted demolition derby' than 'professional investigation.'"

I activated the speaker just as Elijah's crisp voice filled the car: "Phillips."

"It's Jim Butterfield," I said, narrowly avoiding a pothole that seemed to be mounting a hostile takeover of the entire lane. "Is it true Miller found new evidence against Sophie?"

A slight pause, then: "Unfortunately, yes. I was just about to finish convincing Miller to approve her house arrest when one of the officers brought in a letter. Young fellow – looked like he'd spent the night fighting ghosts while questioning his entire understanding of reality."

"Martinez," I sighed, recognizing the description. "What kind of letter?"

"Apparently one where Sophie writes to Maggie, bragging about successfully carrying on her sister's legacy through the Valentine's Day poisoning. Claims this was only the beginning."

"That's complete nonsense," I said, swerving around a squirrel that seemed determined to test both my reflexes and car insurance. Its indignant chittering suggested I'd interrupted some kind of important squirrel business meeting. "Where did they even find this letter?"

"Perhaps I should start from the beginning," Elijah replied. Paper rustled in the background – probably taking notes in a leather-bound notebook that cost more than my car. "When I presented Miller with the receipt, he demanded to know where I got it. Mentioned something about Sophie saying during questioning that it would be in the bottom right drawer of her desk."

"Miller actually remembered that detail?" I asked, impressed despite myself. "Usually he can barely remember where he put his last donut."

"Indeed. I told him the source was irrelevant – the receipt itself provides Sophie's alibi. He disappeared into another room, presumably to make a private call." Elijah's voice carried a hint of amusement. "Though 'private' might be generous, given how his voice carried. Seemed to be berating someone about inadequate crime scene security and sleeping on duty. Something about pastry-based hallucinations."

"Let me guess – he sent Martinez to check that drawer?"

"His exact words were 'Get over there and check that drawer before you start seeing ghost cupcakes again.'" Another rustle of expensive paper. "And that's where they claim they found the letter, mixed in with Maggie's prison correspondence."

"That's impossible," I said, frowning at the darkening sky ahead. "I was there last night – there were only Maggie's letters and the receipt." I thought about the shadow I'd glimpsed near the bakery but kept that detail to myself for now.

"I made a mistake not taking those letters," I admitted. "Never thought they'd be used against her."

"Don't blame yourself," Elijah said smoothly. "You were there for the receipt, not to collect personal items."

"How did they verify Sophie's handwriting?" I asked, steering around another pothole that seemed to have aspirations of becoming a small lake.

"That's the troubling part," Elijah replied. "Miller compared it to the forms she filled out when taking over the bakery – inventory reports, supplier contracts, bank contracts – says the writing is practically identical. Even he could see the match, and I doubt he could tell calligraphy from crayon marks on a good day. Right now he's mostly excited about having evidence that doesn't involve extensive paperwork."

"But how could someone fake her writing so perfectly?"

"That's what we need to find out. Along with who placed that letter in the drawer. Though Miller's more interested in celebrating what he calls 'a simple solution without all that investigative nonsense.'"

The wipers squeaked against the windshield as the snow began falling more heavily. A delivery truck ahead of us was creating an impressive spray of slush that my aging Buick seemed determined to collect.

"What happens now?" I asked. "Can you still get her house arrest?"

"We'll see. Miller's consulting with the county office. I'll do what I can when he emerges from his donut-fueled deliberations. Though his current mood suggests he's already planning a press conference to announce another solved case."

"Let me know if anything changes," I said. "I'm heading back to Oceanview Cove now."

"Did you find anything useful in Rocky Point?"

"A few leads worth following. I'll fill you in in person later."

After ending the call, I glanced at Ginger. "There's something I didn't mention about last night. When we left the bakery, I saw a shadow lurking near the building.

Thought it was just my imagination after such a chaotic day, but now I'm not so sure."

Ginger's whiskers twitched thoughtfully. "A mysterious figure appearing just when incriminating evidence needed to be planted. And someone skilled enough to perfectly forge Sophie's handwriting. I suspect these two mysteries might have the same solution."

"Let's hear what details Emma remembered," I said. "Though I'm hoping for actual evidence rather than cosmic hallucinations about proper pastry alignment."

\*\*\*

The hospital parking lot was significantly emptier than during our morning visit. Most of the Valentine's Day victims had apparently recovered enough to return home, though a few cars suggested some were still dealing with the aftermath. The seagull from earlier had abandoned its post, probably finding more promising targets for aerial criticism.

Sarah intercepted us in the hallway, her teddy bear scrubs somehow looking fresh despite what must have been a long shift.

"Perfect timing!" she exclaimed, already reaching for Ginger. "Ready for your final dose?"

"I hardly think that's nec-" Ginger started, but Sarah had already scooped him up.

"Your blatant disregard for proper feline dignity continues to be concerning," he muttered, though I noticed he didn't struggle very hard against her expert handling.

"I'll have him back shortly," Sarah assured me, cradling a distinctly disgruntled Ginger. "Emma's awake if you want to visit. She's been reorganizing her crystals and muttering about cosmic alignments since she opened her eyes. Something about Neptune's influence on proper pastry display techniques."

I pushed open the door to Emma's room. Shawn sat in his usual chair by the bed, giving me a tired nod as I entered.

I found Emma propped up in bed, surrounded by what appeared to be a carefully orchestrated crystal formation that probably had more strategic planning than most military operations. Her constellation dress continued its gentle twinkling despite its wrinkled state, creating tiny light shows on the ceiling that made the fluorescent hospital lighting look positively mundane. She was adjusting a particularly large rose quartz with the intense focus of someone defusing a bomb made of cosmic energy.

"Welcome back to our world," I said, patting her shoulder.

She launched herself forward with surprising speed, wrapping me in a tight hug that suggested her strength had fully returned. The crystals around her rattled ominously at the sudden movement. "Jim! Thank goodness you're alright! I had such terrible dreams about misaligned pastry displays and improperly positioned napkins!"

"She's been doing that to everyone," Shawn commented from his chair. "Nearly crushed my ribs when she woke up. Though she did predict good tips for the bar next week, so I'll take the bruised ribs as a fair trade."

Emma released me, though her hands immediately returned to adjusting her crystal alignment. "I traveled through the cosmos," she announced, moving a small amethyst exactly three millimeters to the right. "Venus had so much to tell me about proper pastry arrangement. Did you know counter-clockwise dough kneading disrupts the universal harmony?"

I glanced around the room, noticing the absence of Chuck's impressive snoring symphony. "Where's your roommate?"

Shawn chuckled. "Apparently some new intern got his medications mixed up. Chuck went from unconscious to Olympic sprinter in about thirty seconds. Took three nurses to calm him down, but he refused to come back. Said something about not being able to sleep through any more astrological predictions about proper napkin folding."

"His snoring was disrupting the crystal energy field," Emma added seriously, nudging a piece of selenite into what was presumably a more cosmically appropriate position. "Though Mars suggests his running form showed remarkable improvement for someone who spent half a day unconscious."

"Shawn said you remembered something important," I prompted, settling into a chair.

"Oh yes!" Emma brightened, though her hands never stopped their crystal adjustments. A small piece of rose quartz rolled dangerously close to the edge of her bedside table before she rescued it with the reflexes of a cosmic goalkeeper. "The cosmos revealed so much during my journey through the astral plane. Did you know Jupiter's alignment affects the rise of sourdough? And Saturn warns that improper spatula angles create ripples in the cosmic frosting field-"

"Emma," Shawn interrupted gently, catching my eye with a knowing look. "Maybe tell Jim about what happened before the poisoning? When Mr. Edison came to your table? The part that doesn't involve planetary pastry alignment?"

"Oh! Yes, of course." She finally abandoned her crystal arrangement, though her fingers twitched toward them like a musician missing their instrument. "He wanted a reading about his investment plans. Sweet man – always tipped generously, even when the cosmic energies were uncertain. Once left me a twenty just for predicting his parking spot would have positive energy flow."

Her expression softened with the memory. "He was so excited about becoming Sophie's business partner. The stars aligned perfectly for their partnership – except for that slight wobble in Neptune's orbit that suggested possible display case disagreements."

"Business partner?" I leaned forward slightly.

Emma nodded enthusiastically, her bangles creating their usual symphony.

"He loved what she'd done with the bakery – said it was exactly what the town needed. Was going to buy in as co-owner. The crystals suggested great success, though Mars indicated potential disagreements about seasonal decorations. But Venus assured me their pastry vision alignment was strong enough to overcome any minor planetary disruptions..."

"Mrs. Abernathy's hostile takeover theory doesn't seem so far-fetched now," Shawn joked, though his eyes held a serious light. "Though I doubt Mr. Whiskers would make a very effective business partner. His management style seems to consist mainly of napping and judging other people's life choices with that superior look of his."

"Unless he's secretly a financial genius," I replied. "All those hours watching Mrs. Abernathy count cookie inventory might have paid off."

But my mind was already racing ahead, putting pieces together like one of Emma's crystal formations. Mr. Edison's death might not have been just collateral damage – it could have been one of the primary objectives. Someone who knew about his plans to invest, who was familiar enough with his health issues to know exactly what combination of substances would be fatal.

The Valentine's Day poisoning was starting to look less like chaos and more like carefully orchestrated elimination. But who would have known about Mr. Edison's investment plans? And who could have accessed both the bakery and his medical information?

Most importantly – who had the skills to forge Sophie's handwriting so perfectly that even Miller could see the match?

Emma's crystals caught the afternoon light, sending small rainbows dancing across the hospital walls. Her constellation dress continued its gentle twinkling, creating a miniature light show that seemed to match her ongoing murmurs about cosmic alignments and proper pastry karma.

"Venus suggests we should pay attention to unexpected connections," she said, adjusting a piece of amethyst with scientific precision. "Though Saturn warns against making assumptions about proper muffin placement during retrograde."

"The planets seem very concerned about baked goods," I observed, watching her arrange the crystals in what was probably a cosmically significant pattern.

"The universe speaks through many channels," she replied seriously. "Sometimes through pastry alignment, sometimes through proper napkin folding techniques. Though Mars has been particularly vocal about inadequate sprinkle distribution lately."

Through the window, dark clouds began gathering, promising more snow. The weather seemed appropriate somehow – like nature herself was preparing to add another layer to this increasingly complex mystery.

Somewhere in Oceanview Cove, someone was probably feeling very pleased with their plan's execution. They'd managed to eliminate a potential investor, frame Sophie, and throw our entire town into chaos – all while making it look like history repeating itself. A masterful performance of misdirection and carefully planted evidence.

But they'd made one crucial mistake: they'd hurt my friends. And Ginger and I had a particular talent for uncovering the truth that people tried to hide behind carefully crafted lies.

Time to figure out exactly who had orchestrated this Valentine's Day performance – before they decided to arrange an encore.

# Chapter 15

Sarah appeared in doorway, cradling a significantly more relaxed Ginger than the one who'd left with her earlier. His usual precise dignity had softened around the edges, suggesting the medication was already taking effect. The afternoon light caught his orange fur, making him look almost angelic – an effect somewhat undermined by his expression of barely contained indignation.

"All done!" she announced cheerfully. "He's got all his necessary doses. Should be back to full investigative capacity in no time. Though I have to say," she added with a grin, "he's probably the most well-behaved patient I've had all week. Unlike Mr. Thompson, who keeps calling to ask about proper recovery protocols for extended bathroom occupation."

"Her definition of 'necessary' seems remarkably flexible," Ginger muttered, though his usual sharp tone had mellowed to something closer to mild annoyance. "Though I must admit, her proficiency with injections demonstrates considerable skill. Unlike that intern who apparently learned injection protocols from horror movies. I suspect he practices on stuffed animals with disturbingly enthusiastic sound effects."

"Thank you, Sarah," I said, watching how she handled my feline partner with practiced care despite his attempts to maintain a facade of displeasure. Her gentle competence reminded me powerfully of my daughter – they shared that same mix of professional efficiency and natural kindness.

Emma's face lit up at the sight of Ginger, her constellation dress twinkling with increased enthusiasm. Several crystals actually vibrated in response to her excitement. "Bring him here!" she exclaimed, already reaching out with grabby hands that suggested Ginger's dignity was about to take another hit. "Why did you abandon your roomie? The crystal energies were so perfectly aligned! Venus was most displeased by your unauthorized departure!"

"Oh no," Ginger managed, his eyes widening with horror as he realized his fate. "I believe I feel a sudden relapse coming on. Perhaps another dose-" But Sarah was already transferring him into Emma's eager embrace, his protests dying into a resigned sigh that suggested he was mentally cataloging every violation of proper feline handling protocols while simultaneously plotting revenge through strategic furniture scratching.

I couldn't help chuckling at the sight – my usually composed partner trapped in a bear hug by someone wearing twinkling constellations while surrounded by carefully arranged crystals that seemed to pulse in sympathy with his distress. A particularly large rose quartz actually rolled an inch closer, as if offering moral support. Even Sarah smiled, though she tried to hide it behind her clipboard while adjusting her teddy bear scrubs.

"I should get back to my rounds," Sarah said, still fighting a grin. "If you need anything, just check at reception. Though you might want to avoid the third floor – apparently Chuck's still doing laps around the cardiac ward, insisting that Emma's cosmic predictions gave him supernatural running abilities."

Just as Sarah turned to leave, Dr. Chen appeared in the doorway, her practical coat a stark contrast to Emma's cosmic fashion show.

"Mr. Butterfield? A moment?"

Ginger seized the opportunity like a drowning cat spotting a life preserver, somehow extracting himself from Emma's embrace with a move that probably violated several laws of physics. His orange fur stood slightly on end from the static electricity generated by Emma's twinkling dress, making him look rather like he'd just stuck his paw in a light socket.

"The things I endure for this investigation," he muttered as he landed with surprising grace considering the medication, following me into the corridor with as much dignity as one can muster while looking like they'd just lost a fight with a Van de Graaff generator.

"I see our feline investigator is back on his feet," Dr. Chen observed, a small smile touching her usually serious features.

"Can't keep him unconscious for long," I replied. "Bad for his critique schedule."

Dr. Chen's expression turned more serious as she pulled a file from her coat pocket. The folder bore Miller's characteristic donut stains in one corner, suggesting it had survived at least one evidence review session. "I've almost finished analyzing the substances found in Mr. Edison's body. The preliminary results are... interesting."

"Our medical examiner's definition of 'interesting' suggests findings beyond Miller's donut-based investigation techniques," Ginger observed quietly, his fur still attempting to defy gravity from his cosmic encounter with Emma. "Though given our recent experiences, I suppose anything not involving ghost pastries or meditation soundtracks counts as progress."

"As I suspected, there were two distinct substances," Dr. Chen continued, flipping through her notes. Her precise handwriting created neat rows across the page, while Miller's usual scrawl tended to resemble a chicken having an existential crisis while tap dancing. "The laxative was straightforward enough – extra strength, massive quantities. But the other compound..." She frowned slightly, adjusting her glasses. "That's where things get peculiar."

"Peculiar how?"

"It appears to be some kind of knockout drug, but modified – mixed with other compounds in a very specific way. The formulation suggests amateur chemistry, possibly someone working in a makeshift lab. But whoever did it knew exactly what they were doing. The proportions are precise. One wrong measurement could have produced very different results."

The chemical smell from Owen's clothes suddenly clicked into place – not cleaning products at all, but the particular sharp scent of a home laboratory. His garage wasn't hiding a car detailing obsession – it was probably concealing something far more complex. "Could someone set up that kind of operation in a garage?" I asked. "Get these specific results?"

"Your powers of deductive reasoning show remarkable improvement," Ginger commented, his tail twitching with interest despite his still staticky fur. "Though I noticed that chemical aromatherapist's garage setup seemed more Breaking Bad than Good Housekeeping. Unless punk rockers have developed a sudden interest in advanced pharmaceutical studies."

Dr. Chen nodded slowly, her expression thoughtful. "A garage, basement, any space with proper ventilation would work. The equipment isn't particularly specialized. The real trick is knowing the correct formulations." She studied me with sudden intensity, her eyes sharp behind her practical frames. "You have a suspect?"

"Someone with an interesting chemical signature and a suspicious garage," I replied carefully. "Though he's not local. Couldn't have known about Mr. Harrison's medical history – his heart condition that made these substances particularly dangerous."

"Unless he had help," Dr. Chen pointed out, tucking a strand of hair behind her ear. "Mr. Edison wasn't exactly private about his condition – half the town probably knew his medical history. He loved telling people about his heart problems almost as much as he loved talking about his business plans."

"Our punk rock chemist does seem the type to make questionable alliances," Ginger observed, finally managing to smooth his fur back to something approaching normal. "Though his choice in co-conspirators probably depends on their position on proper mohawk maintenance and their tolerance for wallet chains that could anchor small ships."

"Worth investigating," Dr. Chen concluded, tucking her file away in a pocket. "Especially given the precision of the formulation. This wasn't random – someone knew exactly what effect these substances would have on someone with Mr. Harrison's condition."

"Thank you," I said. "This helps a lot."

"Always happy to assist someone who actually looks at the evidence," she replied with a meaningful look. "Rather than filing it under 'Too Much Paperwork.'"

Back in Emma's room, we found Shawn had acquired coffee from somewhere. The rich scent of dark roast mixed with the antiseptic hospital smell, creating an oddly comforting combination that almost masked Emma's latest attempt at burning sage for proper crystal alignment.

I filled them in on our morning adventures in Rocky Point, describing Owen's suspicious behavior and his chemical-laden garage. When I finished, Shawn leaned forward with interest.

"Dr. Chen's findings suggest our friendly neighborhood punk might be moonlighting as an amateur chemist," I explained, settling into a chair. "Complete with garage laboratory and suspicious pink car."

"Like Breaking Bad meets Hot Topic?" Shawn asked, grinning. His bartender's instincts for reading people had clearly picked up on Owen's carefully crafted rebellion during my description. "Though I'm guessing his lab set-up involves more skull decorations and fewer scientific principles."

"More like Breaking Badly Dressed," Ginger muttered, having reclaimed a safe distance from Emma's enthusiastic crystal arrangements. "Though his chemical experimentation might explain that hair color. I doubt that particular shade of purple exists in nature without significant molecular manipulation."

"We should check out that garage," Shawn said, his expression turning more serious. His years of handling rowdy bar patrons had given him a sixth sense for potential trouble. "I could come along – add some muscle in case your punk friend decides to get creative with his chemistry set. After all, I've had practice dealing with people who think their bad decisions qualify as performance art."

I smiled, remembering Owen's scrawny frame beneath all those chains and spikes. He looked like he'd lose a fight with a strong breeze, let alone an actual confrontation. "Think I can handle him if needed. Though I appreciate the offer. His most dangerous weapon seems to be his inability to maintain basic lawn care."

"Venus suggests strength in numbers during planetary alignment," Emma added helpfully, now arranging her crystals in what appeared to be a scale model of the solar system. A particularly large amethyst had been designated as Jupiter, while a small piece of quartz orbited it like a crystalline moon. "Though Neptune warns against judging combat effectiveness based on hair volume. And Saturn has strong opinions about proper motorcycle part arrangement in front yards."

My phone chose that moment to unleash what sounded like a gospel choir performing an interpretive dance version of "Stayin' Alive," complete with what might have been Emma's attempt at backup vocals. Elijah's number flashed on the screen.

"Phillips here," his crisp voice carried the particular urgency of expensive litigation. The background sounds suggested he was in his sleek black BMW – the same one

I'd admired on my porch this morning. "We need to meet. Soon. There have been... developments."

"What kind of developments?"

A slight pause, followed by what sounded like his car's navigation system suggesting a route with unreasonable optimism. "They're transferring Sophie to county tomorrow morning. Miller's washing his hands of the whole thing – claiming it's beyond local jurisdiction now. He seemed particularly pleased about reducing his paperwork load."

"Jesus," I muttered, running a hand through my hair. "He got exactly what he wanted – less paperwork and a simple solution he can pass off to someone else. Probably already planning which donut shop to celebrate at."

"Precisely why we need to meet," Elijah replied, his tone suggesting he shared my frustration with Miller's dedication to avoiding actual police work. "Preferably somewhere that serves lunch – I haven't eaten since I drove to Oceanview Cove this morning. My blood sugar is dropping faster than Miller's interest in proper investigation."

"I know just the place," I said. "Rose's café near the harbor? Ten minutes? Their chowder might make up for Miller's negligence."

"I'll GPS it," Elijah replied, then ended the call, probably already calculating billable hours for lunch.

"At least someone can successfully operate navigation technology," Ginger observed dryly, his feline hearing having caught every word of the phone conversation.

"Though I notice his confidence suggests unfamiliarity with local road work and seasonal potholes. His German engineering might meet its match in our town's creative approach to street maintenance."

"Got to run," I told Shawn and Emma. "Keep me posted if anything changes here. Especially if Chuck breaks his own running record."

"The bar later?" Shawn asked. "Fill us in on whatever you learn? Though maybe we should check the drinks for suspicious substances first."

"Where else?" I smiled. "Hopefully with fewer poisonings this time. And maybe fewer mayoral bathroom occupations."

"Jupiter suggests moderate consumption during cosmic investigations," Emma called after us as we headed for the door. "Though Saturn approves of proper garnish alignment in all beverages! And Mars insists that lemon wedges must face northeast during Mercury's retrograde!"

***

Through the hospital's entrance doors, a pink minivan with out-of-state plates caught my attention, it looked suspiciously familiar. The minivan sat trying to appear inconspicuous between a delivery truck and what appeared to be Miller's backup donut procurement vehicle.

"Isn't that the same minivan from this morning?" I asked Ginger, watching how it seemed to sink lower in an attempt to appear invisible, like a teenager caught somewhere they shouldn't be.

"Indeed," he replied, whiskers twitching with interest. "The paint does bear a remarkable resemblance to that pink car in Owen's garage. Unless multiple people in this area share his questionable taste in automotive aesthetics."

The minivan's engine roared to life as soon as we emerged from the hospital doors, producing a sound that suggested either mechanical distress or an attempt at intimidation. It peeled out of the parking lot with the particular urgency of someone who's just remembered an extremely important appointment on the other side of town, or possibly someone who's realized their surveillance technique needs work.

"That's got to be our chemical enthusiast," I said, already reaching for my keys. "We could probably catch-"

"Meeting first," Ginger interrupted firmly. "The lawyer awaits, and I suspect he's not the type to appreciate tardiness due to impromptu minivan chasing. His hourly rate probably exceeds the value of that entire vehicle. Besides, by the time you start the engine of your ancient Buick, that van will be halfway to Rocky Point. We'll have plenty of future opportunities for automotive pursuit. Probably with better lighting and less hospital parking lot navigation required."

The winter afternoon had begun its slow fade toward evening as we walked to my car, the sky taking on the particular shade of gray that suggested more snow.

"Meeting first," I agreed, unlocking the door of my car. "Then we see what other chemical mysteries our punk friend is cooking up in that garage of his."

"Assuming he hasn't already relocated his laboratory to more fashion-forward premises," Ginger commented as we navigated around a pothole that seemed to be attempting to achieve sentience. "Though I suspect his dedication to that particular shade of pink suggests a certain commitment to location. That, or a remarkable inability to choose subtle automotive colors. Perhaps we should consult Emma about proper vehicle pigmentation during planetary alignment."

The afternoon traffic moved steadily around us as we headed toward Rose's, carrying us toward whatever new complications awaited. But at least we had a solid lead now – a suspicious minivan, a makeshift laboratory, and a punk rocker with questionable chemical hobbies.

The list of clues kept growing, but we needed more – and quickly. Preferably before Sophie found herself explaining everything to county investigators who probably shared Miller's enthusiasm for simple solutions over actual investigation. I just hoped Elijah had some good news to balance out the complications. Though given how this Valentine's Day had gone so far, I wasn't going to hold my breath. Unless, of course, we ended up back in Owen's garage – in which case holding my breath might become a survival strategy rather than a metaphor.

# Chapter 16

The February wind cut sharply across the café's parking lot as I pulled in beside Elijah's sleek BMW. Salt and slush from the winter roads had transformed my Buick's once-blue paint into a modern art installation of varying grays, while his vehicle gleamed like it had never encountered weather more severe than gentle spring rain. The contrast between our cars was almost comical – his German engineering masterpiece crouched like a predatory cat next to my battle-scarred veteran that had weathered more winters than I cared to count.

"Ah, the eternal struggle between old and new," Ginger observed as we exited the car, his tail swishing thoughtfully. "Though I notice your ancient chariot maintains a certain dignified persistence, like a librarian refusing to retire despite the advent of e-books."

"She's gotten me everywhere I needed to go," I defended, patting my car's hood affectionately. The metal felt cold under my gloved hand, decades of faithful service condensed into that simple touch. "Even found all those chicken coops in Rocky Point this morning."

"Yes, your vehicular adventures in poultry navigation continue to impress," Ginger replied. "Though Elijah's car probably comes with GPS that actually knows the difference between Manitoba and Maine."

The café's windows glowed invitingly against the deepening afternoon, steam fogging the glass where it met the winter air. The warmth within created patterns in the condensation that looked like abstract art, occasionally disturbed by the movement of customers inside. Through the clouded panes, I could see Elijah already seated at a corner table, engaged in what appeared to be far more than a simple order-taking interaction with Rose. Her usual efficient demeanor had softened into something that suggested his legal charm worked on more than just judges.

The bell above the door announced our arrival with its familiar chime. The café's warmth wrapped around us, carrying the mingled aromas of Rose's famous chowder, fresh coffee, and that particular scent of a place that's served comfort food to generations of locals. The wooden floor creaked beneath my feet, its boards worn smooth by countless footsteps. Mrs. Nelson occupied her regular window table, still looking pale from yesterday's Valentine adventure, though that didn't stop her from tackling a massive sandwich with determination.

"I see you've met Rose," I said as we approached their table. Elijah's expensive suit looked almost exotic against the café's well-worn comfort, like an orchid blooming in a vegetable garden. A half-empty cup of coffee suggested he'd been waiting long enough to sample Rose's specialty roast.

"Indeed," he smiled. "I took the liberty of ordering chowder for us both. Rose has been telling me fascinating stories about local maritime history."

"And a saucer of cream for our feline investigator," Rose added with a wink, already moving toward the kitchen. "Premium stuff today – we just got a new dairy delivery."

"Her standards for dairy products suggest hidden expertise," Ginger commented, watching Rose disappear into the kitchen. "Though I notice the quality of cream often improves proportionally to the number of solved cases. Perhaps we should investigate more frequently."

I settled into the chair across from Elijah, the old wooden frame creaking beneath my weight. Old photographs lined the walls around us – decades of local fishing crews, weather-beaten faces smiling out from behind glass that needed dusting. A particular image caught my eye – Mr. Edison accepting some kind of community award, his face beaming with pride. The sight sent an uncomfortable pang through my chest.

"Mr. Phillips-" I began, but he held up one manicured hand.

"Please, it's Elijah. I think we're beyond formalities at this point, don't you? Especially after our shared experience with Miller's unique approach to law enforcement."

I nodded, watching how his fingers absently adjusted his perfectly straight tie. A habit born of countless courtroom appearances, probably. "Jim, then. What exactly happened after Miller made that call to county?"

"Nothing good," Elijah sighed, his polished demeanor cracking slightly. "He strutted out of his office like a rooster who'd just discovered dawn, announced Sophie's transfer was set for tomorrow morning, then proceeded to organize his donut collection by filling type. All my arguments for house arrest might as well have been delivered in Sanskrit for all the attention he paid. I swear he was more concerned about whether to file maple bars under 'M' for maple or 'B' for bar."

"That sounds like Miller," I agreed. "Once he thinks he's found a simple solution, trying to change his mind is like convincing a seagull to adopt table manners. Though I suspect the seagull might be more open to new ideas."

"Which brings us to whatever evidence you've managed to uncover," Elijah said, leaning forward slightly. His watch caught the café's warm light. "We've got until tomorrow morning to find the real culprit before Sophie joins the county's finest in their charming concrete accommodations."

Rose appeared with our chowder, the steam rising in delicate spirals that carried promises of comfort. A small saucer of cream accompanied the bowls, which Ginger examined with his usual critical assessment of dairy products.

"The presentation suggests proper respect for feline dining standards," he observed, settling into a more comfortable position. "And the saucer's placement indicates someone familiar with proper cream-to-whisker clearance ratios."

"This is extraordinary," Elijah said after his first spoonful, genuine surprise coloring his voice. "And at these prices... I have clients who pay ten times as much for food half this good."

"Told you," I smiled, watching him recalibrate his understanding of small-town cuisine. The chowder's rich aroma filled our corner of the café, mixing with the ever-present scent of coffee and fresh-baked bread.

I filled him in on our Rocky Point investigation, watching his expression shift from professional interest to focused concern. The missing footage, Owen's suspicious behavior, the chemical smell from his garage – each detail adding another layer to our growing case. When I mentioned Dr. Chen's analysis and the shadow I'd glimpsed near the bakery, his fingers stilled on his spoon.

A pair of regulars passed our table, discussing yesterday's Valentine's Day chaos in hushed tones. Their theories had evolved to include international pastry spies and something about coded messages in cookie arrangements – Mrs. Henderson's influence clearly reaching far beyond her front porch.

"The pink minivan's probably his too," I added once they'd moved out of earshot. "Same color as the car in his garage. We've seen it twice near the hospital today, like it's following us. Not exactly subtle about it either – unless there's suddenly a high demand for suspicious vehicles in pink."

"A solid lead," Elijah nodded thoughtfully, dabbing his mouth with a napkin. "But his motivation seems unclear. And how did he access the bakery during preparation? From what I understand, Sophie runs a tight ship when it comes to kitchen access."

"That's just it," I said, lowering my voice as another couple of locals passed our table. "I think he had help. Someone local who knew about Edison's condition, his investment plans. Someone with access to the bakery."

"Any thoughts on who?"

Two names flashed through my mind – Brenda with her precise measurements and obsessive attention to detail, Mrs. Abernathy with her decades of baking knowledge and connection to every aspect of town life. But surely not... The thought felt wrong, like finding a typo in a familiar book.

"After months of solving cases together, I can read your suspicions like an open book," Ginger commented quietly. "And I must admit, our potential suspects share a concerning dedication to proper pastry protocol."

"I don't know-" I started, but movement outside the window caught my attention. That same pink minivan rolled past, moving from the parking lot toward the street with suspicious casualness. The driver's silhouette was just visible through the tinted windows, their mohawk a dead giveaway despite their attempt at stealth.

"There it is again," I said quietly, nodding toward the window. "Definitely following us. Unless punk rockers have suddenly developed an interest in small-town cafés."

Elijah stood in one fluid motion, dropping several bills on the table – enough to cover ten bowls of chowder, let alone our two. "Then let's follow it. We can't lose this lead."

"He knows my car," I said, already rising. The chair scraped against the floor, the sound unnaturally loud in the quiet café. Mrs. Nelson looked up from her sandwich, raising an eyebrow at our hasty departure. No doubt this would feature prominently in tomorrow's gossip session with Mrs. Henderson, probably evolving to include international car chases.

"But not mine," Elijah smiled, a predatory gleam in his eye that suggested his BMW wasn't just for show. He headed for the door with the particular urgency of someone used to seizing opportunities.

I hadn't planned on riding in a luxury sports car today, but plans seemed increasingly flexible lately. The leather seats welcomed us with expensive comfort as we settled in – though with only two doors, Ginger had to perch on my lap like some kind of orange throw pillow with opinions.

"The interior suggests less 'car' and more 'spacecraft,'" he observed, taking in the array of gleaming controls and soft ambient lighting. "Emma would probably declare it cosmically aligned with Jupiter's automotive chakras."

The engine purred to life with a sound that made my Buick's starting routine sound like an asthmatic chainsaw attempting opera. Elijah guided us smoothly into traffic, maintaining careful distance from our quarry while navigating around a crater-sized hole in the pavement.

The evening had settled fully now, transforming the town's familiar streets into corridors of shadow and lamplight. The minivan ahead moved with the particular casualness of someone trying very hard to appear like they weren't being followed, taking turns that suggested either aimless wandering or poorly executed evasion techniques.

As we passed the "Leaving Oceanview Cove" sign, it became clear the minivan was heading toward Rocky Point.

"Dear God, what do you people do to your roads out here?" Elijah exclaimed as we hit another pothole. "I've seen smoother terrain on off-road rally courses!"

"Welcome to small-town charm," I chuckled.

"I see our rural infrastructure fails to meet Bavarian engineering standards," Ginger commented dryly. "Though I must say, these potholes do add a certain dramatic flair to our pursuit. Like an impromptu obstacle course designed by someone with a grudge against German automobiles."

My phone's ring cut through the tension – an unknown number flashing on the screen. The sound startled me enough that I nearly dropped the device, which would have probably activated every meditation app Emma had installed simultaneously.

"Mr. Butterfield!" a familiar voice exclaimed when I answered, the enthusiasm practically vibrating through the speaker.

"Jenny? Is that you?"

"The convenience store clerk," I explained quickly to Elijah, who gestured for me to put it on speaker while expertly maneuvering around what appeared to be the grand canyon's smaller cousin masquerading as a pothole.

"Yes!" Jenny's enthusiasm crackled through the speaker. "I found your number online – googled 'Oceanview Cove private investigators' and found all these articles about your solved cases in the Gazette's website. You're like local heroes or something! The Christmas case was amazing – though that photo of you after saving the tree, all red-faced but relieved, probably wasn't your most dignified moment."

I made a mental note to have a word with the Gazette's photographer about their editorial choices.

"Then I checked the business listings and there it was – Oceanview Cove Investigators. Your cat looks so professional in his photo. Is that a tiny detective badge he's wearing?"

"A regrettable costume choice that shall never be mentioned again," Ginger muttered, his tail twitching at the memory.

Elijah gestured impatiently with one hand while the other guided us smoothly around yet another pothole. I steered the conversation back on track. "What made you call at this hour?"

"Oh! Right!" Jenny's excitement rose another notch. "So I couldn't stop thinking about that missing footage, right? And I have this friend who's amazing with computers – total geek, but in a good way. Like, he once hacked the high school cafeteria menu to list 'existential dread' as the daily special. After my shift, I convinced Ralph to let us stay late, and my friend managed to restore the deleted section! Whoever tried to erase it was totally amateur hour – like using white-out on a computer screen level of amateur."

"What happened in those missing ten minutes?" I asked, watching the minivan's taillights ahead as we navigated another stretch of pockmarked road. The vehicle's pink paint caught occasional flashes from passing streetlights, looking increasingly familiar with each glimpse.

"So Owen's just finishing his burrito – which looked seriously questionable, by the way, like maybe it had achieved sentience – when this woman comes in wearing a baseball cap. She flips the 'Open' sign to 'Closed' – which got them arguing at first, probably because Owen hadn't finished communing with his potentially radioactive lunch. But then they settle down, and Owen starts messing with the computer like he's trying to hack NASA, but with more hair gel."

"The eternal struggle between punk rock and proper point-of-sale protocol," Ginger observed quietly.

"A few minutes later," Jenny continued, her voice carrying the particular excitement of someone sharing prime gossip, "he scans like ten packs of laxatives and prints her receipt. My friend says he definitely changed some settings in the register program to make the customer name appear on that fake receipt."

"Did you recognize her?" I pressed, noticing how Elijah's hands had tightened slightly on the steering wheel.

"She kept her head down most of the time, trying to avoid the camera like she was auditioning for a spy movie – but not, you know, a good spy movie. But right at the end, she looks up for just a second – like, right into the lens. Then she must have noticed because she turns away super fast, points at the camera while saying something to Owen. But that second was enough."

"Jenny," I said, probably more sharply than intended. The suspense made my stomach tighten, or maybe that was just lingering effects from yesterday's Valentine's Day adventure.

Her answer dropped into the car's quiet interior like a stone into still water:

"Brenda Evans. The waitress from Silver Spoon Diner. No doubt about it. Same face that serves me slightly burned toast every Sunday morning while lecturing about proper temperature gradients in bread cooking."

The silence that followed felt heavy enough to measure. Even the BMW's engine seemed to purr more quietly, as if processing this revelation. Ahead, the minivan's taillights continued their steady progress toward Rocky Point, unaware that our pursuit had just become significantly more complicated.

"Well," Ginger said finally, his tail twitching thoughtfully against my knee, "I suppose this adds new meaning to the phrase 'killer customer service.' Though I notice Brenda's dedication to precise measurements has taken a rather dark turn."

# Chapter 17

Jenny's words hung in the BMW's quiet interior, each one clicking into place like tumblers in a lock. Brenda Evans. Of course. The pieces of the puzzle suddenly aligned with such clarity that I wondered how I'd missed it before.

Her previous attempts to open a bakery – all those failed loan applications she had mentioned, each rejection probably stoking a slow-burning resentment. The impressive chocolate work on those Valentine's treats that showed she had the skill to forge Sophie's handwriting, her obsessive precision making her a natural forger. Her fixation with exact measurements matching perfectly with Dr. Chen's analysis of the carefully calculated poison – someone who counted cookie crumbs wouldn't make mistakes with chemical substances.

Her temporary position at the bakery gave her the perfect cover and access. She'd played it masterfully – the efficient assistant, carefully hiding her true intentions behind a flour-dusted apron and precise measurements. Owen had probably been just a pawn in her game – providing the garage for her makeshift lab, helping with the fake receipt, planting that letter in Sophie's desk.

And most crucially, she'd been right there in the kitchen alongside Sophie and Mrs. Abernathy, able to slip those substances into the treats while maintaining her careful facade of efficiency. Her obsession with exact measurements would have made adding precise amounts of poison as natural as measuring vanilla extract.

"Thank you, Jenny," I said into the phone's speaker, my voice steady despite the rush of realizations. "Could you email me that footage? The address should be on the Gazette's website along with my number."

"Oh yeah, it's right here!" Jenny's enthusiasm crackled through the speaker.

"Could you keep the original footage safe?" I asked. "We'll need it."

"Of course!" Jenny's voice practically vibrated with excitement. "I'll guard it with my life! This is so cool – helping real private investigators! Like in those TV shows, but with better cats! My cats are going to be so impressed when I tell them! Though Sir Fluffington might be jealous – he's been trying to solve the mystery of where I hide his treats for months."

After ending the call, I couldn't help smiling at her enthusiasm. In Jenny's world, we were probably something between superheroes and those detectives from her favorite TV shows. Well, maybe we were, in our own small-town way. Though I doubted most TV detectives had to deal with ghost pastries and cosmic playlists.

"Brenda?" Elijah asked, expertly navigating around another pothole that looked deep enough to have its own ecosystem. His expensive suspension made the crater feel like a gentle dip, unlike my Buick's interpretation of such encounters as personal offenses. "Sophie mentioned that name. Her temporary assistant?"

I filled him in quickly – explaining how all the pieces fit together, watching his expression grow more focused with each detail. The expensive leather of his steering wheel creaked slightly under his tightening grip as I described Brenda's likely motivations and methods.

"It fits," he agreed finally. "Though we should get a proper confession from our punk rock friend first. Clarify his role in all this before he decides to start another band and skip town."

"Looks like we'll get our chance," I said as Owen's minivan pulled into his driveway ahead of us. "He's home."

My phone chimed with an email notification. The sender's name – *"CrazyCatLady2002"* – could only be Jenny. The subject line read *"SUPER SECRET SPY FOOTAGE (!!!)"* with enough exclamation points to suggest her keyboard had gotten stuck.

"Perfect timing," Elijah murmured, parking his BMW with smooth precision that made my usual parking attempts look like interpretive dance performed by someone who'd just discovered the concept of steering wheels.

Owen emerged from his minivan just as Ginger and I exited Elijah's car, his mohawk slightly wilted from the winter humidity and what appeared to be excessive nervous sweating. Various chains jingled discordantly as he moved, like wind chimes designed by someone with a grudge against melody. His eyes widened when he spotted us, face shifting from surprise to irritation faster than Miller could spot a donut.

"You again?" he called out, his wallet chain creating a nervous symphony that probably counted as percussion in his failed band. "What, are you following me now? Nice car upgrade from this morning, by the way. Guess private investigating pays better than I thought. Though the color's a bit boring – could use some skull decals, maybe some flames..."

His attempt at casual bravado shattered the moment Elijah stepped out of the driver's side. The sight of an impeccably dressed lawyer emerging from a luxury vehicle had an immediate effect – Owen's face transformed from punk rock defiance to pure panic with impressive speed.

"I wouldn't advise running," Elijah said smoothly as Owen's hand twitched toward his minivan's door. The casual authority in his voice froze Owen mid-movement, his numerous chains creating a final jingle of defeat.

"Our friend seems to have developed a sudden appreciation for proper legal representation," Ginger observed quietly. "Though I notice his fight-or-flight response favors neither his mohawk maintenance nor his wallet chain acoustics. Perhaps we should have Emma check if running from lawyers aligns with his astrological chart."

Elijah approached Owen with measured steps while tapping something on his smartphone. I smiled slightly, noting that at least with smartphones we were equals – his sleek device looked as much a technological nemesis as my own.

"Owen," Elijah began, his voice taking on that particular tone lawyers use when they know they've already won, "we have some rather interesting evidence regarding your involvement in recent criminal activities. I suggest we discuss your options for minimizing the inevitable consequences. Unless you'd prefer to explain everything to the county judge – I hear he's particularly fond of creative sentencing involving community service and proper lawn maintenance."

Owen attempted to rally his rapidly crumbling punk rock persona, though his mohawk seemed to be wilting in real time. "What evidence? You can't just show up on my property talking about crimes and-"

"Jim," Elijah interrupted smoothly, "perhaps you could show our friend the security footage?"

I fumbled with my phone, trying to find Jenny's email. Instead, my finger somehow activated a notification from YouTube, and suddenly the quiet street filled with what sounded like an entire monastery attempting to achieve enlightenment through aggressive chanting, accompanied by what might have been yak bells.

"Turn that racket off!" a voice shouted from a nearby window, where an elderly woman in curlers glared down at us. "Some of us are trying to watch our soaps! The handsome doctor is about to reveal his evil twin!"

Another window opened. "Is this one of them flash mobs? In my day we just had regular mobs, and we liked it that way!"

"Interesting music taste," Elijah commented mildly while I fought with the volume controls. Emma's latest "cosmic playlist" suggestions had apparently infiltrated my recommended videos with alarming efficiency.

"The eternal struggle between technology and dignity continues," Ginger sighed as I finally silenced the impromptu Tibetan concert. "Though I must say, your ability to accidentally activate spiritual soundtracks shows remarkable consistency. Perhaps we should market it as a new form of meditation – 'Unexpected Enlightenment: Finding Inner Peace Through Technological Incompetence.'"

I managed to locate Jenny's email and handed the phone to Elijah, who held it at a careful distance while playing the footage for Owen. The punk rocker's face went through several interesting color changes as he watched his past self conspiring with Brenda – impressive given the number of piercings that had to accommodate each new shade.

"That's impossible," he whispered, his wallet chain jingling with nervous energy that suggested it might be considering a solo career. "I deleted that part myself! Used three different delete buttons and everything!"

"Deleted footage can be restored," Elijah replied. "And I think you understand what this means for your immediate future. Unless you'd prefer to discuss it with the FBI's cybercrime division?"

Owen's shoulders slumped, his carefully crafted rebellion crumbling like day-old pastry. The numerous studs on his jacket caught the glow from nearby street lamps, creating a disco ball effect that seemed inappropriately festive for the moment.

"It was all Brenda," he said quietly. "She... she got into my head. Like one of those mind control experiments, but with better baking skills."

"Start from the beginning," Elijah prompted. The winter wind caught Owen's mohawk, making it wave like a surrendering flag.

"I used to hang out at the Silver Spoon Diner a lot," Owen began, absently adjusting a skull-shaped belt buckle that had probably seen better days. "Got to talking with Brenda. She seemed... interested, you know? Said she liked my style, my rebellious spirit. Even said my band's name was 'delightfully anarchic' – should've known something was up right there. Nobody likes the name 'Toxic Hamster Revolution' unless they want something."

"Our friend's taste in romantic partners suggests questionable judgment," Ginger commented. "Though I notice his ability to recognize manipulation arrives fashionably late, much like his understanding of proper lawn maintenance. That gothic flamingo appears to be judging his life choices with remarkable accuracy."

"When she got the temporary job at Sophie's, she got really excited," Owen continued, his numerous rings catching the light as he gestured. "Started talking about this plan – said we could make history, called it the 'bakery takeover of the century.' Said she'd make me her business partner once she took over."

"After Toxic Hamster Revolution's third failed album – creative differences with the bassist, plus our drummer discovered meditation and renamed himself Moonbeam – being a business partner sounded pretty good. So I helped her. Let her use my garage for her 'experiments.' Faked that receipt, deleted the footage. Even planted that fake letter in Sophie's desk. Then I found out someone had died from the poisoning. It got real, you know? And Brenda... she changed. Started having me follow the detective dude and his cat around in my pink minivan – not exactly subtle spy work, but she insisted. Had to report everything back to her. She was scared they'd figure it out."

"And were you supposed to report today's activities?" Elijah asked carefully.

Owen nodded, creating a ripple effect through his mohawk that suggested his hair gel was fighting a losing battle with gravity. "Was heading home to call her now. Though I guess that plan's kind of shot, unless jail cells come with good reception these days?"

"That can wait," Elijah said smoothly. "First, show us this garage laboratory of yours. I'm particularly interested in seeing what a punk rock chemistry setup looks like."

Owen hesitated only briefly before leading us inside. The garage interior carried that sharp chemical smell I'd noticed earlier, emanating from a makeshift lab setup that looked like a high school chemistry classroom had collided with a Hot Topic stockroom and neither had walked away unscathed. Beakers and test tubes shared space with skull decorations and band posters featuring names that appeared to be randomly generated combinations of dark adjectives and questionable nouns – "Midnight Hamster Apocalypse" seemed to be Owen's latest musical venture.

A black light in one corner cast an eerie purple glow over what appeared to be a shrine to failed band merchandise – t-shirts with increasingly desperate designs, demo CDs with hand-drawn covers, and a stack of flyers advertising performances at venues that probably didn't exist anymore. A guitar with more stickers than strings leaned precariously against a wall, its strap decorated with safety pins that suggested tetanus shots should be required before handling.

"Did you help create the substance?" Elijah asked, studying the setup with professional interest while carefully avoiding contact with anything that might stain his impeccable suit.

"Nah, that was all Brenda. Wouldn't even let me in here while she worked. Said the measurements had to be exact." Owen kicked an empty energy drink can, sending it skittering across the floor to join what appeared to be a growing collection. "She got really intense about it – kept muttering about proper chemical ratios and sweet revenge. Started calling herself the 'Queen of Precise Measurements' which was kind of weird, but I figured it was just a baker thing."

"His definition of 'just a baker thing' suggests remarkable flexibility," Ginger observed, eyeing a particularly aggressive-looking skull decoration that appeared to be judging his fur maintenance. "Though I notice his threshold for suspicious behavior appears calibrated to Hot Topic employee standards."

"So... what happens now?" Owen shifted nervously, his boots scuffing against the concrete floor. "Are you really FBI? Like, proper FBI with sunglasses and everything, not just really well-dressed private investigators?"

"Something like that," Elijah replied smoothly, brushing an imaginary speck of dust from his sleeve. "And your situation might be... negotiable. Provided you continue cooperating. Wait here a moment – try not to start any new bands while we're gone." He gestured for me to follow him outside.

Owen remained in his garage, surrounded by the evidence of both chemical experimentation and questionable life choices, looking remarkably like one of his own band posters – lost, slightly confused, and in desperate need of better career advice.

Once outside, I turned to Elijah. "About that negotiation – was that just to keep him calm, or can you really help reduce his sentence?"

Elijah checked something on his phone before responding. "Let's just say his quick cooperation might work in his favor. But he's still an accomplice – judge might go easier on him than Brenda, but he's not walking away from this." He glanced at the garage where Owen waited, surrounded by his sad attempt at a chemistry lab and what appeared to be a graveyard of failed band merchandise. "Right now, though, we need to focus on Brenda. Take my car, go to her house. See if you can get a confession."

He held up his phone, showing the screen's recording app paused mid-session. My eyebrows rose. "You recorded everything?"

"Of course. Best evidence is what they say themselves." He pocketed the phone with practiced smoothness that suggested years of courtroom theatrics.

"What about Owen while I'm gone?" I asked.

"I'll call the local police – hopefully they're more competent than Miller. They can deal with Owen and help retrieve that camera footage from Jenny." He paused. "Now, about Brenda. Just approach her carefully at first. Be friendly, lead her toward admitting it. Given your success with previous cases, I trust you can handle this. Though maybe avoid commenting on her chocolate tempering technique – bakers can be sensitive about that."

"Sophie's sister Maggie tried to strangle me in my living room," I reminded him, absently rubbing my neck at the memory. "Any suggestions for avoiding a repeat performance with her apparent protégé?"

"Stay alert, keep recording, and maybe don't mention her failed bakery attempts," he said with a slight smile. "And don't forget to start the recording."

"That might actually be harder than getting the confession," I muttered, thinking of my ongoing battles with technology. "Unless Emma's installed some helpful apps about proper evidence collection during Mercury's retrograde."

"Just don't mess it up," he said, then gestured toward his car. As I turned to leave, he called out, "Oh, wait – you might need these." He pulled out his keys, the expensive fob gleaming in the winter light like it was made of actual precious metals.

"I should warn you," I said, accepting them with more reverence than they probably required, "I haven't driven anything newer than my Buick since the Carter administration. Your car might be slightly out of my technological comfort zone."

"Don't worry about it," he replied with casual affluence that suggested car insurance was a foreign concept. "I have two more at home. Just try to avoid any major potholes – German engineering has standards."

\*\*\*

The BMW's interior welcomed us back with expensive leather and that particular new car smell that probably cost extra. Every surface gleamed with the kind of precision that suggested a team of engineers had spent years perfecting the exact angle of each button. The dashboard displayed more information than my office laptop, including several readings whose purpose I couldn't begin to guess.

Ginger settled into the passenger seat this time, arranging himself with obvious appreciation for the premium upholstery. He tested various positions like a critic at a luxury furniture showroom, finally settling into what appeared to be an optimal configuration for both comfort and judgmental observations.

"I must say, German engineering does have its advantages," he observed, kneading the leather experimentally. "The fabric tension-to-comfort ratio suggests remarkable attention to detail."

I started the engine, and the dashboard lit up like a spacecraft's control panel. Lights I'd never seen before blinked into existence, displaying information about everything from tire pressure to the current phase of the moon. The car responded to the slightest touch of the accelerator with enough enthusiasm to make my heart jump and Ginger's claws extend reflexively into the premium leather.

"Perhaps I should fasten my seatbelt," Ginger commented as we pulled away from Owen's house with slightly more acceleration than intended, narrowly missing his gothic flamingo. "This could be an interesting interpretation of high-performance driving. Though I suspect even Emma's planetary alignments couldn't predict our trajectory."

# Chapter 18

"Perhaps we should establish some ground rules about velocity control," Ginger suggested as we narrowly avoided becoming permanently acquainted with Owen's mailbox. "Though I notice your relationship with high-performance vehicles mirrors your success with smartphone operations – enthusiastic but lacking finesse."

The car's countless gauges and displays created a light show worthy of Emma's cosmic fashion sense. Half the indicators seemed to be warning me about things I didn't understand, while the other half appeared to be judging my technique. A helpful screen suggested I was either drastically exceeding optimal fuel efficiency or accidentally engaging warp drive.

"You know," I said, wrestling with a steering wheel that seemed to interpret suggestions as mere guidelines, "I'm starting to miss my Buick's more... relaxed approach to acceleration."

"Your ancient chariot's inability to achieve speeds beyond 'leisurely stroll' does have certain advantages," Ginger agreed as we encountered our first major pothole.

The BMW's sophisticated suspension transformed what would have been a bone-jarring crash in my car into a gentle bounce, though several warning lights suggested the vehicle was filing formal protests with the department of transportation.

The roads between Rocky Point and Oceanview Cove had apparently decided winter was the perfect time to reinvent themselves as obstacle courses. Patches of ice gleamed with malicious intent in the fading light, while large potholes lay in wait like asphalt predators.

"I believe that last crater just applied for township status," Ginger observed as we swerved around a particularly ambitious example. "Though I must say, your attempt at high-speed pothole avoidance resembles a drunken ballet performed by someone who just discovered what feet are."

The BMW's GPS, unlike my phone's creative interpretation of navigation, actually seemed to know where we were going. Its cultured voice offered directions with the particular patience of someone explaining simple concepts to a particularly dense student. Though I noticed it had developed a slight edge of concern after watching my third attempt at what it probably considered a basic turn.

"Recalculating," it announced with what sounded suspiciously like a sigh. "Please attempt to maintain the correct lane. And perhaps consider taking a performance driving course."

A patch of ice sent us into an impromptu dance that probably violated several laws of physics. The BMW's various safety systems engaged, though I could have sworn I heard them muttering German expletives under their mechanical breath.

"Your interpretation of winter driving techniques continues to push the boundaries of automotive innovation," Ginger commented as we regained our intended direction. "Though I suspect this isn't quite what the engineers had in mind when they designed those stability controls."

We passed the "Welcome to Oceanview Cove" sign at an angle that suggested we were either entering town or auditioning for a drift racing competition. The BMW's traction control light flickered with what felt like personal judgment.

Finally pulling up to Brenda's house felt like completing an Olympic event. I parked with perhaps more enthusiasm than the situation required, causing several of the BMW's assistance systems to engage simultaneously in what felt like an intervention.

"Well," Ginger observed as the car settled into stillness, various warning lights slowly fading, "I believe we've successfully redefined several aspects of German engineering. Though I suspect Bavaria's finest mechanics are experiencing unexplained anxiety right now."

\*\*\*

The winter darkness had settled around us, shadows stretching across Brenda's meticulously maintained yard.

Her porch light illuminated the front steps with theatrical timing, making the walk to her door feel like approaching center stage. My hand felt unnaturally heavy as I reached for the knocker.

Brenda answered almost immediately, as if she'd been waiting. Her apron bore traces of fresh flour, and the scent of baking cookies drifted from behind her. Everything about her appearance suggested business as usual, except for the slight tightness around her eyes when she spotted the BMW.

"That's quite a vehicle," she said, her voice carrying forced casualness. "Quite a change from your previous car."

"Just borrowed it," I replied, watching how her gaze kept drifting to the vehicle with what looked like recognition. "Still partial to my Buick, even if it does remember the Carter administration."

Her eyes landed on Ginger, and something flickered across her face – too quick to read but enough to notice. "And look who's recovered! Such a relief. We were all so worried." The warmth in her voice had all the sincerity of a plastic plant.

"Would you like to come in?" she asked, stepping back from the doorway. "I've got cookies almost ready. Perfect timing, really."

"That would be great," I said, following her inside. The house felt different now, knowing what we knew. Every precisely arranged item seemed less about organization and more about control.

"Make yourselves comfortable in the living room," she called over her shoulder, already heading for the kitchen. "Tea? I've got several varieties."

"Black is fine," I replied, settling onto the sofa. Ginger arranged himself beside me with careful dignity, his tail twitching slightly as he surveyed the room.

The wall of bakery plans caught my eye immediately. The designs had evolved since yesterday, becoming more detailed, more precise. She'd probably been updating them, confident that Sophie's imminent transfer to county jail would clear the path for her takeover.

"Our aspiring baker seems remarkably optimistic about her future business prospects," Ginger murmured, following my gaze.

"She knows why we're here," I replied quietly, watching the doorway for Brenda's return. "Her whole demeanor screams guilty knowledge. That comment about the BMW wasn't just casual observation."

Before Ginger could respond, Brenda returned with a tea tray. Each item had been arranged with mathematical precision – cups exactly parallel, spoons aligned at perfect angles. She set a cup before me with the careful movements of someone who'd measured the exact distance between cup and saucer.

"Would Ginger like some milk?" she asked, her smile not quite reaching her eyes.

"Absolutely not," Ginger muttered. "I'd sooner drink from Mrs. Henderson's bird bath."

"That would be nice," I said smoothly, ignoring Ginger's scandalized expression.

As Brenda disappeared back into the kitchen, Ginger turned to me with obvious disapproval. "Have you completely lost what remains of your investigative judgment? Accepting beverages from a known poisoner suggests either remarkable bravery or profound foolishness."

"We need to maintain the illusion," I whispered. "Why would a cat refuse milk unless we suspected something?"

"Perhaps because we arrived in a vehicle that screams 'dramatic confrontation'?" Ginger replied dryly.

While Brenda was occupied in the kitchen, I pulled out my phone. By some miracle of timing or cosmic intervention, I managed to activate the recording function on the first try. Emma's meditation apps remained mercifully silent as I put the device on the sofa beside me.

"Will wonders never cease," Ginger observed. "Though I suspect this technological victory merely ensures some future catastrophic failure. Probably involving accidentally broadcasting Tibetan throat singing during the confession."

Brenda returned with a delicate china saucer of milk, setting it before Ginger with the same precise movements she'd used for the tea. Ginger made a show of sniffing it before turning away with exaggerated disdain.

"Cats and their standards," Brenda laughed, though the sound held an edge sharper than her kitchen knives. "So particular about their food, aren't they? Now, what brings you by? Any progress with the case?"

I leaned back, adopting a casual posture I didn't feel. "Actually, yes. Though some developments are concerning. They're transferring Sophie to county tomorrow morning."

"Oh no, really?" Brenda's expression shifted into what probably passed for concern in acting classes. "I meant to visit her at the station but got so caught up with baking. Such a shame, isn't it? All this evidence pointing to her following Maggie's path..."

"Speaking of evidence," I said carefully, watching her reaction, "there are some interesting questions about timing. Like where certain people were when that receipt for laxatives was issued."

"Oh?" Her hands moved to adjust an already perfectly straight doily. "That does sound intriguing. I was probably at the Silver Spoon during that time – my old shift pattern, you know. Though it feels like ages ago now."

The lie rolled off her tongue with practiced ease, but her fingers betrayed her – constantly adjusting, arranging, controlling her environment as she tried to maintain control of the situation.

A timer chimed from the kitchen, the sound slicing through the tension. "Oh! The cookies are ready," Brenda exclaimed, rising with perhaps too much enthusiasm.

"You simply must try them. My stress-baking has really improved my technique."

As she disappeared into the kitchen, Ginger stood with fluid grace. "I believe I'll conduct a brief reconnaissance. Something about those cookies suggests more than just improved technique."

He padded silently after Brenda while I sat trying not to look like someone recording a confession. The tea in its precise cup seemed to watch me with the same judgment as the BMW's warning lights.

Ginger returned with remarkable speed, his tail puffed with alarm. "Two trays," he reported quickly. "Identical cookies, but she's separating them onto different plates with surgical precision. Unless she's developed an obsession with cookie symmetry that rivals her measurements, something's very wrong."

"You think she's added-"

"Substances to one batch? Given her recent history of creative baking additions, I'd say that's a safe assumption."

Before we could discuss further, Brenda returned bearing two plates. The cookies on each looked exactly identical – same size, same golden brown color, same precise arrangement. Even the plates matched perfectly, down to the delicate floral pattern around the edges. She placed one plate decisively on my side of the coffee table, the other on hers.

"Those cookies are definitely enhanced with more than just vanilla extract," Ginger said quietly. "The plates are identical – she'll never notice if you switch them while I create a distraction. Though I suspect my dignity may not survive what I'm about to do."

Before I could question his plan, Ginger launched into action. He leaped onto a shelf containing Brenda's meticulous collection of recipe boxes, sending several teetering dangerously close to the edge. The effect was immediate – Brenda lunged forward with a small cry of distress, her hands outstretched toward her precious organizational system.

"No, no, bad kitty!" she called out, rushing to prevent recipe chaos. "Those are arranged by category and sub-category!"

While she was occupied trying to prevent cross-contamination between bread and pastry recipes, I reached forward with trembling hands. The plates felt unnaturally heavy as I quickly switched their positions, terrified of making any noise that might give away the maneuver.

"Those are organized by rising time and flour type!" Brenda's voice carried real panic now as Ginger threatened a box labeled 'Sourdough Variations (Advanced)'. She finally managed to scoop him up, holding him away from her precious collection. "Naughty boy!"

I tried to look innocent as she returned, still cradling a suspiciously cooperative Ginger. I gave him a slight nod, and he immediately extracted himself from Brenda's grip.

"Well," Brenda said, smoothing her apron and settling back into her chair, "shall we try the cookies? This batch has the perfect ratio of butter to flour – I've been experimenting with the percentages."

She selected a cookie from her plate (previously mine) and took a delicate bite. "Just right," she declared. "Proper measurements make all the difference."

I picked up one from my plate (previously hers), noting how her eyes tracked the movement with barely concealed anticipation. "These are excellent," I said truthfully – because they were. The flavor and texture showed real skill, making it even more tragic that such talent had been turned toward darker purposes.

"Thank you," she beamed, though the expression didn't quite reach her eyes. "Stress-baking has really helped me process everything that's happened. Though I do wish the circumstances were different."

I sipped my tea, watching her over the rim of the cup. Time to move this along – whatever she'd added to those cookies would be taking effect soon, and I needed that confession recorded.

"Actually," I said carefully, setting down my cup, "I received something interesting today – a security video that suggests some people weren't exactly where they claimed to be when that fake receipt was issued."

Brenda's hands froze halfway to another cookie. "Oh?" Her voice aimed for casual but landed somewhere between strained and panicked.

"Yes – very clear footage from the Ready Mart. Shows someone who looks remarkably like you working with

Owen on that receipt." I watched her face carefully, wondering if I'd need to actually show her the video to get a confession.

I needn't have worried. Her carefully maintained facade crumbled faster than an underbaked cookie. "That idiot," she muttered, shaking her head. "I told him to delete it properly. But no, Mr. 'I know all about computers because I can work the cash register' couldn't handle a simple security system."

"So it was you," I said quietly. "You orchestrated the entire Valentine's Day poisoning."

A bitter laugh escaped her, reminding me unnervingly of Maggie. "Well done, Sherlock. You found your culprit. Though I have to say, I expected it to take longer. You got sloppy with that car though – I recognized it from Sophie lawyer's visit to the police station."

"Why?" I asked, hoping my phone was still recording. "Why take this path? You have real talent, Brenda."

"Talent?" Her voice carried years of frustration. "Talent doesn't get you anywhere in this world. Not without connections, without someone giving you a chance." Her hands clenched in her lap. "As I told you yesterday – all those rejected loan applications, Maggie's dismissal of my skills... One comment about my chocolate tempering technique and she wouldn't even consider me as her assistant."

She stood suddenly, pacing with precise steps that suggested she'd measured the exact distance between furniture. "Taking over the bakery this way was my only option. And it was perfect – everything measured exactly, timed precisely. Those substances were so easy to add while we worked. Sophie and Mrs. Abernathy were so caught up in their baking zen, they never even noticed."

"And Mr. Edison?" I asked quietly. "Was his death part of your plan?"

"Actually, no," she admitted, her voice carrying no remorse. "That was just lucky timing. Sophie mentioned his investment plans that morning while we were preparing the treats. Said she was 'seriously considering his offer.'" Her laugh held no humor. "Talk about killing two birds with one stone – or two competitors, in this case. I didn't even know about his heart condition, but it worked out perfectly."

"What exactly was in those treats?" I asked, watching how her hands kept moving, adjusting, controlling her environment even as she confessed.

"Oh, that was clever," she said, pride creeping into her voice. "Found the formula on one fascinating forum – mixing knockout drops with other compounds to create something special. The laxatives were just for chaos, really. I just added both randomly to different treats. Even those pet ones – sorry about that," she added, not sounding sorry at all.

"And Owen following us around town?"

"Had to keep an eye on your investigation somehow. That pink minivan isn't exactly subtle, but Owen's not exactly mastermind material." She shrugged. "After you visited yesterday, I knew I needed more evidence against Sophie. That letter was easy – her handwriting is so predictable. Basic calligraphy principles, really."

"You seem awfully willing to confess everything," I observed, noting how she kept glancing at my midsection – probably waiting for signs of digestive distress.

"Why not?" A smile spread across her face. "The laxatives should be kicking in right about now. Then the other effects will start. I'll have plenty of time to decide what to do with you after you emerge from the bathroom and pass out."

Before I could process that last part, she doubled over with a sharp gasp. Her eyes darted to the cookie plates, widening with sudden understanding. "You switched them," she whispered. "When did you–" Another cramp hit, making her straighten with panic. "You switched the plates!"

She lurched toward me, hands outstretched like a cartoon villain's last desperate attempt. But another cramp doubled her over, and she rushed from the room with a string of surprisingly creative curses that suggested her vocabulary wasn't limited to baking terms.

"Did she just try to strangle me?" I asked Ginger, listening to the bathroom door slam followed by sounds suggesting Brenda was having an intensely personal conversation with her plumbing.

"Indeed," he replied. "Though I notice her attempt at villainous assault lacked Maggie's dedication to proper strangulation technique. More like an interpretive dance of evil intentions."

A particularly loud crash from the bathroom suggested Brenda had discovered that precise measurements didn't help much in certain situations.

"What did she mean about passing out?" I asked, but the words came out slightly slurred. The room had begun to tilt in interesting ways, and my thoughts felt like they were moving through molasses.

"Jim?" Ginger's voice carried uncharacteristic concern. "The tea. She must have-"

But I couldn't focus on his words anymore. The room spun lazily around me as darkness crept in from the edges of my vision. My last coherent thought was profoundly irritating – after all our careful switching of cookie plates, I'd completely forgotten about the tea.

From the bathroom came more creative cursing and what sounded like someone learning advanced yoga poses the hard way, but the sounds seemed increasingly distant.

The darkness claimed me just as Ginger's voice faded into what sounded like a very sarcastic observation about my beverage choices. Some things, it seemed, remained constant even as consciousness didn't.

Mrs. Henderson would have quite the story for her front porch updates tomorrow – assuming I woke up to hear them.

# Chapter 19

The bakery glowed with warmth against the winter evening, its windows fogged with steam from fresh-baked treats. Inside, Sophie's Valentine's Day decorations transformed the space into something magical – delicate paper hearts catching light like snowflakes, red ribbons dancing in the gentle air from the ovens. The scent of butter and vanilla wrapped around us like a familiar embrace.

Martha sat across from me at our usual table, laughing at something I'd said. Her eyes sparkled with that particular joy she always found in small moments. Sunlight streaming through the windows caught the silver strands in her dark hair, making them shimmer as she reached for another croissant.

"You have to try this one," she insisted, breaking it in half to reveal perfect layers of buttery pastry. "Sophie's really outdone herself." Steam rose from the fresh-baked treat, carrying promises of comfort and home.

"Remember our first Valentine's Day?" she asked, brushing crumbs from her blue sweater – the one I'd given her that Christmas, the color perfectly matching her eyes. "When you tried to surprise me with homemade chocolate truffles but they turned out more like chocolate rocks?"

"Hey, it's the thought that counts," I protested, smiling at the memory. "Besides, you still ate them all."

"Every single one," she agreed, reaching across the table to squeeze my hand. "Though I think I chipped a tooth on that last one."

We lingered over our coffee, watching other couples drift in and out of the bakery. Emma waved from her table where she was conducting Valentine's Day fortune readings with her crystal collection. The afternoon light played through the windows, creating pools of warmth on the well-worn floor.

"We should go for a walk," Martha suggested finally, wrapping her scarf around her neck – the hand-knitted one with tiny hearts that her mother had made years ago. "The beach will be beautiful with fresh snow."

The transition from the bakery's warmth to the winter air took my breath away, but Martha's hand in mine kept me anchored. We made our way down the familiar streets, past shops decorated for Valentine's Day, their windows glowing with welcoming light.

The beach stretched before us, pristine and untouched. Our footprints marked the fresh snow as we walked along the shore, the winter ocean stretching gray and endless beside us. Waves whispered secrets against the shore, their rhythm as steady as a heartbeat. Martha had always loved the beach in winter – said it felt more honest somehow, stripped of summer's pretenses.

"Beautiful day for a walk," she said, squeezing my hand. Her voice carried that warmth that had first drawn me to her, that gentle strength that had kept me anchored through life's storms. The wind caught her hair, making it dance around her face as she smiled up at me.

The sun hung low on the horizon, painting the snow-covered beach in shades of rose and gold. Seabirds wheeled overhead, their calls carrying across the winter silence. Martha's face glowed in the fading light as she turned to me, about to say something...

But the scene dissolved like sugar in hot tea, replaced by harsh fluorescent lighting and the particular antiseptic smell that belongs exclusively to hospitals. Sarah's face swam into focus above me, her teddy bear scrubs suggesting I hadn't dreamed myself completely out of reality.

"Welcome back," she said warmly, adjusting something on the IV stand beside my bed. "You had quite a few people worried, though I suspect none more than your feline partner over there."

I turned my head – slowly, since the room seemed inclined to spin – toward the window. Ginger sat on the sill in a patch of late morning sun, attempting to look both dignified and completely unconcerned about my awakening.

"How long was I..." I gestured vaguely at the hospital bed, which felt like it had been constructed specifically to make comfort impossible.

"Just overnight," Sarah replied, checking various monitors. "Though given recent events, I'd say you've earned the rest. Not everyone manages to solve a mass poisoning case and then become a victim of the culprit's backup plan all in one day."

"About that," I said, trying to piece together memories that felt like fragments of a jigsaw puzzle scattered by a particularly enthusiastic toddler. "What happened exactly? Last thing I remember was Brenda's creative cursing from her bathroom."

Sarah's smile widened slightly. "From what I understand, you can thank your partner for the timely rescue." She nodded toward Ginger, who somehow managed to look even more smugly disinterested. "Apparently he somehow managed to call Sophie's lawyer from your phone. Mr. Phillips realized something was wrong and sent help. Though I hear they had to wait quite a while for Ms. Evans to emerge from her own bathroom crisis before they could properly arrest her."

"Our town certainly has an interesting history with aggressive bakers," I observed, noting how the morning sunlight created patterns on the hospital room's floor that reminded me uncomfortably of the Valentine's Day decorations from my dream.

"That's putting it mildly," Sarah agreed, adjusting my pillows with the particular efficiency of someone who's mastered the art of making institutional bedding slightly less torturous. "But this case sets a new standard for creative criminal techniques. Who would have thought precise measurements could be used for evil?"

I glanced around the familiar hospital room. "I see they put me in Emma's room."

"Yes – and you had visitors this morning," Sarah said, adjusting her teddy bear scrubs, which today featured the bears having what appeared to be a picnic in a snow-covered forest. "Mr. O'Connell and Mr. Reeves stopped by – the latter smelling strongly like he'd taken an impromptu swim in the harbor. Emma insisted on coming too, even though she just got released yesterday evening. Said something about needing to ensure proper cosmic alignment of your recovery."

"That sounds like Emma," I smiled. "I'll catch up with them later."

"I'll let you rest," Sarah said, heading for the door. Her teddy bears seemed to wave goodbye as she disappeared into the hallway.

Once we were alone, I turned to Ginger. "Alright, partner. Time to fill me in on what really happened."

"Ah, so Sleeping Beauty finally wishes to hear the tale," he replied, stretching languorously in his patch of sunlight. "Though I notice your unconscious state lasted significantly longer than my brief medical vacation. Perhaps we should consult Emma about proper cosmic alignment during poisoned tea consumption."

"Skip the commentary and start with what happened after I passed out," I said, though I couldn't help smiling at his familiar sarcasm.

Ginger settled into a more comfortable position, his tail curling around his paws with precise dignity. "Well, after your rather dramatic collapse – which, I must say, lacked the theatrical grace one expects from proper swooning – I immediately took action. First priority was securing that recording of our amateur baker's confession."

"You stopped the recording?"

"Indeed. Managed to reach your technological nemesis without disturbing your impromptu nap. Though I suspect the accompanying soundtrack of Brenda's creative cursing from the bathroom added a certain dramatic flair to the evidence."

He paused to groom one paw, though I noticed his usual precise movements seemed slightly sluggish with fatigue. "Then came the real challenge – contacting our well-dressed legal ally. Thankfully, his number appeared in your recent calls, and the phone's screen remained mercifully upward."

"You actually called Elijah?"

"What else was I supposed to do? Wait for Miller to finish organizing his donut collection by frosting type?" Ginger's whiskers twitched with mild irritation. "Though I will admit, attempting to communicate urgent messages through meowing presents certain linguistic challenges. Fortunately, our lawyer friend possesses more deductive reasoning skills than our local law enforcement."

Outside, the winter sun climbed higher in the sky, its rays growing more intense. Through the window, I could see the parking lot filling with visitors' cars, each one carrying someone else's story of illness or healing.

"The sirens arrived shortly after," Ginger continued. "The medics showed remarkably more efficiency than Miller's usual response time – though I suppose a sleeping hamster could outpace our local police response. The medics' initial attempts to wake you proved about as successful as your average interaction with smartphone settings."

"And the police?"

"Ah, that's where things became interesting. Not our usual donut-enthusiast law enforcement, but actual competent officers from Rocky Point. Though I must object to their Sheriff's suggestion about 'getting the cat out of the crime scene before he messes anything up.' Rather offensive to a feline investigator of my caliber."

A knock at the door interrupted Ginger's narrative. The sound carried a particular authority that suggested expensive suits and legal expertise. Sure enough, Elijah appeared, looking as impeccably dressed as ever despite the early hour. Sophie followed, her face showing both relief and lingering traces of her ordeal in the police cell.

"I see our sleeping detective has finally rejoined the conscious world," Elijah observed.

"How are you feeling?" Sophie asked, her face showing genuine concern. She looked tired but relieved, the strain of her jail time visible in subtle ways – a slight slump to her usually perfect posture, shadows under her eyes that spoke of sleepless nights on an institutional mattress.

"Better now that I see that you're free," I replied. "Though I seem to have missed all the exciting parts. Care to fill me in on how everything unfolded?"

"Your partner deserves most of the credit," Elijah said, nodding toward Ginger. "When I received that call from your phone, hearing only insistent meowing, I knew something had gone wrong. Not that cat calls are typically part of my legal practice."

"Our resourceful feline friend's communication skills proved remarkably effective, despite certain species-related limitations," he continued, absently adjusting his perfectly straight tie. "I immediately contacted emergency services and the Oceanview Cove police. Though I was in Rocky Point at the time, dealing with Owen's arrest."

"Which reminds me," Sophie interjected, "how did that work out?"

"The Rocky Point Sheriff took charge of Owen's situation personally," Elijah replied. "Two officers escorted him to the station while the Sheriff and three others accompanied me to Brenda's house. We arrived to find the medics already attending to Jim, but the local law enforcement was conspicuously absent."

"Probably still organizing their response by donut preference," Ginger muttered.

"The evidence on your phone proved invaluable," Elijah continued. "Thankfully, your lack of password protection – which I should mention is a significant security risk – worked in our favor. The recording of Brenda's confession was clear enough to convince even the most skeptical officer."

"Though they did have to wait quite a while for her to emerge from her bathroom crisis," Sophie added, a slight smile touching her lips. "Apparently her own poisoned cookies proved remarkably effective."

"Indeed," Elijah agreed. "While the officers maintained what they termed a 'bathroom perimeter', the Rocky Point Sheriff and I headed straight to the Oceanview Cove police station. We arrived just as Miller and his team were preparing to respond to the initial call – which, I might add, had been placed nearly forty minutes earlier."

"The shame of being outpaced by out-of-town law enforcement seemed to affect Miller's usual enthusiasm for simple solutions," Elijah continued, his expression suggesting he'd found some satisfaction in that particular development. "Though it still took several hours of explaining from both myself and the Rocky Point Sheriff before Miller agreed to contact the county office about Sophie's release."

Sophie shook her head slightly, her hands twisting in her lap. "I still can't believe it was Brenda all along. I was even considering offering her a permanent position as second assistant when Alice returns."

"I tried to give her a chance," Sophie continued quietly. "Even though having two assistants would have strained the budget. And all that time, she was just..." She trailed off, unable to find words for such calculated betrayal.

"What happens now?" I asked. "With the bakery?"

"I'm going to take some time before reopening," Sophie replied, her voice steadying as she discussed practical matters. "Wait for Alice to return, maybe even offer Mrs. Abernathy a consultant position. People need time to forget about being poisoned on Valentine's Day before they'll trust our treats again. Familiar faces might help restore that trust."

"I'll miss your croissants in the meantime," I said. "Will you join us at the Salty Breeze tonight? The usual post-case gathering."

Sophie shook her head, a small smile touching her lips. "Not tonight. I need some time to process everything. Two days in a cell gives you a lot to think about." She gave me a pointed look. "Besides, you should be resting, not hanging out in bars after being poisoned."

"On the contrary," I argued, "there's no better medicine than drinks with friends, listening to the town's latest theories about the case. I'm sure Mrs. Henderson has already crafted several elaborate scenarios involving secret recipes and mysterious midnight bakers."

"Well, we won't keep you from your recovery then," Sophie said softly. "We still need to give some final statements at the station. Apparently, Miller requires everything in triplicate when admitting he was wrong."

"More like avoiding paperwork until the last possible moment," Elijah added, rising with his usual smooth grace. "Though I suspect he's currently reorganizing his filing system to include 'Bakery-Related Crimes: Advanced Edition.'"

After they left, the hospital room felt quieter somehow. Morning sun streamed through the windows, creating long rectangles of light across the floor. In one, Ginger had arranged himself with his usual precise dignity, though I noticed his eyes kept drifting closed despite his attempts to appear alert.

"I think I'll take a short nap," I said, feeling the lingering effects of both poison and interrupted sleep. "Need to be fresh for the Salty Breeze tonight."

"A wise decision," Ginger agreed, not bothering to open his eyes. "Though I assure you, my own rest is purely to maintain optimal investigative capabilities. Not at all related to spending a sleepless night monitoring your unconscious state."

"Did you really stay up all night watching over me?"

"Don't be ridiculous," he muttered, his tail curling closer around him. "I merely conducted periodic wellness checks between essential naps. Pure professional courtesy."

But as sleep began to claim me again, I noticed the dark circles under his eyes told a different story. My last thought before drifting off was how fortunate I was to have a partner who'd deny losing sleep to watch over me – even when the evidence was written clearly in his tired eyes and unusually subdued sarcasm.

Some truths, it seemed, were best left unspoken between friends. Even if one of those friends happened to be a particularly opinionated cat with a talent for solving mysteries and saving his human partner from poisoned tea.

# Chapter 20

The evening air held a crisp winter bite as Ginger and I walked toward the Salty Breeze. Streetlights cast warm pools across the snow-dusted sidewalks while my phone's screen glowed with Sarah's contact information. I'd promised to call her once the case was solved, and given recent adventures with poisoned tea and dramatic confessions, this definitely counted as "solved."

"Let's hope your technological nemesis behaves for this particular call," Ginger observed as I dialed. "Though I notice your success rate with phone operations suggests we should prepare for either impromptu meditation music or possibly an emergency alert about proper cosmic alignment during family conversations."

Sarah answered on the second ring. "Dad! I was hoping you'd call. Did you figure out who poisoned everyone at the bakery?"

"Actually, yes. Just wrapped up the case today. Well, technically last night, though I spent most of today unconscious in the hospital-"

"The hospital?" Sarah's voice jumped an octave. "What happened? Are you okay?"

"I'm fine now," I assured her quickly. "Just a slight encounter with some poisoned tea during the culprit's confession. Ginger managed to call for help – though I'm still not entirely clear on how he operated my phone with paws."

"Dad! You can't just casually mention being poisoned like you're talking about the weather! Start from the beginning – what happened?"

I filled her in on the details – Brenda's elaborate plan, Owen's makeshift laboratory, the switched cookie plates, and my own encounter with poisoned tea. Sarah listened with growing amazement and concern.

"I can't believe you solved it so quickly," she said when I finished. "Though I probably shouldn't be surprised – you and Ginger do have a knack for uncovering the truth. Even if it means occasionally getting poisoned in the process."

"You sound surprised by our efficiency. Are you questioning our investigative abilities?"

"Of course not!" She laughed, the sound carrying echoes of Martha's. "But you certainly seem to attract more than your fair share of criminal bakers."

"Actually, speaking of the case – I had the strangest dream while I was unconscious. About your mother."

"Oh?" Sarah's voice softened.

"We were at Sophie's bakery, celebrating Valentine's Day. Your mother was laughing about those disastrous chocolate truffles I tried making for our first Valentine's together – you know the story?"

"The truffles that could have been classified as lethal weapons? Mom used to say they were probably harder than diamonds. She ate every single one though."

"She did." The memory warmed me despite the winter chill. "In the dream, we walked along the beach afterward. Everything felt so real – the snow, her hand in mine, that blue sweater I gave her..."

"The one that matched her eyes," Sarah finished quietly. "I remember that sweater. She wore it until it practically fell apart." A pause, then: "It's a shame you never got to spend Valentine's Day in Oceanview Cove with Mom. She would have loved spending her retirement in her hometown."

"She would have solved half these cases before breakfast," I agreed. "Probably while correcting everyone's grammar and telling me to stand up straighter."

Sarah laughed. "Definitely. Though I bet even she wouldn't have predicted your second career as a small-town detective with a cat for a partner."

The Salty Breeze's warm glow appeared ahead, golden light spilling onto the snowy sidewalk. Inside, I could see familiar silhouettes gathering for our usual post-case celebration.

"I should go," I said reluctantly. "Time for the traditional gathering of theories and tall tales. I'm sure Mrs. Henderson has already developed several involving secret pastry syndicates and coded messages in cookie arrangements."

"Have fun, Dad. You've earned it. Just... maybe check your tea for suspicious substances first?"

"Very funny. Love you, sweetheart."

"Love you too, Dad. Give Ginger a scratch behind the ears for me – assuming his dignity can handle such familiarity."

***

The familiar warmth of the Salty Breeze wrapped around us as we entered, carrying the mingled scents of beer, fried food, and decades of spilled drinks soaked into worn floorboards. The usual evening crowd had already settled in, their conversations creating a comfortable backdrop of small-town life.

A cheer went up when we stepped inside. Chuck raised his glass from his corner table, his face showing no signs of his earlier running adventures through hospital corridors. Several other Valentine's Day victims approached, hands extended in congratulation.

"If you're looking to thank someone," I said as they crowded around, "shake paws with my partner here. Without his quick thinking and creative phone skills, Brenda might have escaped. Well, once she managed to leave her bathroom anyway."

"Your modesty remains remarkably intact for someone who survived both poisoned cookies and compromised tea," Ginger observed as the crowd dispersed. "Though I notice you neglected to mention your own creative interpretation of German automotive handling during our investigation."

Mrs. Abernathy sat at her usual table, Mr. Whiskers maintaining his regal pose beside her despite his recent adventures in outdoor facilities. Her eyes met mine across the room, carrying a weight of responsibility I recognized all too well.

"Shall we pay our respects?" I suggested to Ginger.

"I don't see why we should-" Ginger started, but I cut him off.

"Did I forget to mention that our imperial friend spent quite some time investigating the landscaping options behind various bushes? Apparently even Persian nobility isn't immune to Brenda's chemical additions."

Ginger's whiskers twitched with sudden interest. "You mean to tell me that pompous pile of fur experienced the same undignified fate as the mayor? Why didn't you mention this crucial detail earlier?" He was already moving toward their table, tail held high with anticipation.

Mrs. Abernathy's face showed genuine warmth as we approached, though shadows of recent events lingered in her eyes. "Mr. Butterfield, Ginger – I'm so glad you're both recovered. Those hours waiting at the hospital felt endless."

"You visited?" I asked, settling into a chair while Ginger arranged himself with precise dignity, his gaze fixed on Mr. Whiskers with newfound interest.

"Of course. Though you were quite thoroughly unconscious at the time. Sarah – the nurse, not your daughter – kept us updated on your condition." She adjusted an already perfectly aligned napkin. "I feel I owe you both an apology. If I hadn't recommended Brenda to Sophie..."

"Don't," I said firmly. "You couldn't have known what she was planning. None of us could."

"Perhaps. But after Maggie..." She trailed off, hands still moving restlessly across the table's surface. "I should have been more careful about who I trusted with Sophie's bakery."

"You did trust the right person with Alice," I reminded her. "She already proved herself to be an excellent assistant before Liam's accident."

Her expression brightened slightly. "She certainly did. Such a gentle soul, and her piping technique is remarkable. The bakery hasn't been the same without her. I do hope she returns soon."

While we talked, Ginger had initiated what appeared to be a complex territorial negotiation with Mr. Whiskers. Their usual silent standoff carried new undertones now, with Ginger's tail twitching in barely contained amusement.

"I don't suppose your recent outdoor adventures provided any cosmic insights?" I heard him ask quietly.

"Though I notice your usual dignity seems somewhat diminished by memories of botanical exploration."

Mr. Whiskers' only response was to groom one paw with exaggerated precision, though his ears flattened slightly at the reference to his garden experiences.

"Sophie mentioned you might consult at the bakery," I said, drawing Mrs. Abernathy's attention back from watching the feline drama unfolding beside us. "Help restore people's trust in the place."

"She did mention it," Mrs. Abernathy nodded. "Though I'm not sure... after everything that's happened..."

"Sometimes the best way forward is to keep doing what you do best," I suggested. "In your case, that's knowing everything there is to know about proper baking technique and not being shy about sharing that knowledge."

A small smile touched her lips. "I suppose someone needs to ensure proper croissant lamination standards are maintained. And Sophie's oven temperature control could use some refinement..."

"Time to join our friends," I said to Ginger, noting how Shawn was already preparing my drink and reaching for the premium cream. "Though I'm sure you and Mr. Whiskers have plenty more to discuss about proper feline dignity during times of digestive crisis."

"Indeed," Ginger replied, his tail still twitching with barely contained amusement. "It seems his usual imperial bearing lacks its usual authority when combined with memories of emergency shrubbery investigation."

The evening crowd had settled into their usual patterns as we made our way to the bar. Emma's crystal collection caught the warm light, sending tiny rainbows dancing across the counter. Her constellation dress seemed to have acquired even more twinkling lights since her hospital stay, as if she'd decided additional cosmic illumination might prevent future poisoning attempts.

"Our intrepid investigators return!" Shawn called out as we approached, already sliding my usual drink across the counter. "And looking remarkably healthy for someone who spent the morning unconscious."

"Couldn't miss our traditional post-case gathering," I replied, settling into my usual stool while Ginger claimed his spot with practiced dignity. "Besides, I'm eager to hear the latest theories spreading through town."

"Oh, you'll love this one," Shawn grinned, polishing a glass with practiced efficiency. "Mrs. Henderson is convinced Brenda and Owen are actually undercover agents from a rival tourist town, sent to destroy Oceanview Cove's bakery reputation. Apparently, there's a whole conspiracy involving secret recipes and midnight baking circles."

"A modern Bonnie and Clyde," Robert added from his seat beside Emma, "if Bonnie was obsessed with proper measurements and Clyde couldn't maintain basic lawn care. Though they didn't quite manage to pull off even one successful crime."

"The stars knew they were doomed to fail," Emma declared, adjusting a particularly large crystal that seemed to pulse in the bar's warm light. "Venus was completely misaligned with proper criminal activities during Mercury's retrograde. And my unconscious cosmic journey clearly revealed their karmic imbalance."

"Of course it did," Shawn agreed with the particular patience of someone who'd learned not to argue with Emma's celestial insights. "Though I suspect your crystal arrangements had less to do with their capture than Ginger's creative phone skills."

"I still wish I'd been there to help," Robert said, his face showing genuine regret. "Instead of chasing fish while you were chasing criminals."

"Speaking of which," I said, accepting the drink Shawn placed before me, "how did that big order work out?"

"Caught plenty," Robert nodded, satisfaction creeping into his voice. "Though I missed all the excitement. Quite ironic really – Brenda wanting nothing more than to run the bakery, while Maggie just used it as a stepping stone to her dreams of luxury. Both willing to poison people for their ambitions."

"Different paths to the same tragic end," I agreed. A moment of silence fell over our small group as we remembered Mr. Edison.

"Well, this cocktail certainly won't win any awards for proper technique," Mrs. Abernathy's voice carried from her table. "The garnish alignment is completely haphazard, and don't get me started on the ice-to-liquid ratio."

"Everyone's a critic," Shawn called back good-naturedly. "Though I notice you haven't stopped drinking it."

"Speaking of drinks," Robert said, his expression shifting to something more serious, "you might want to stock up, Shawn. Word is we're getting a boat racing tournament in a month."

"A what?" Emma's crystals actually vibrated with her surprise.

"Some rich guy from the city picked our harbor for a county-wide racing competition. Says our scenery's perfect for it." Robert's eyes lit up with the particular enthusiasm of someone who loves boats in all their forms. "Should bring quite a crowd."

"In March?" I asked skeptically. "Won't there still be ice?"

"That's actually perfect," Robert explained, warming to his topic. "The ice in these parts always melts by early March. The water will still be clear but the weather will still be cool. Not like summer when the heat makes everyone crazy. Plus," his grin widened, "there's a hundred thousand dollar prize for the winner."

"A hundred thousand?" The words came from several voices at once, mine included.

"That kind of money could attract some dangerous competitors," I said thoughtfully, already seeing potential problems.

"Indeed," Ginger observed quietly, his face emerging from the saucer of cream with a telltale white droplet on his nose. "And large cash prizes often inspire creative interpretations of racing regulations. Perhaps we should prepare for our next case – assuming you've recovered from your adventures in poisoned beverage consumption."

The evening continued to deepen around us, conversations flowing as naturally as Shawn's drinks. Through the windows, snow had begun falling again, drifting past the warm glow of the windows. Each flake caught the warm light from inside, creating tiny moments of brightness against the darkness.

But somewhere beyond that peaceful scene, wheels were already turning. A hundred thousand dollars could make people do desperate things – I'd seen enough cases to know that truth well. Next month's boat race would bring more than just competitors to our quiet harbor.

For now though, we had this moment – friends gathered together, sharing warmth against the winter night, while outside the snow continued to fall, each flake carrying the promise of both beauty and danger. Spring would bring new adventures soon enough.

"To solved cases," Shawn raised his glass in a toast. "And to whatever comes next."

We all lifted our glasses, even Mr. Whiskers managing to look dignified despite Ginger's continued commentary about proper feline bathroom etiquette. The drinks caught the light like liquid gold as we brought them together.

"To whatever comes next," we echoed, though something told me our next case might already be sailing toward us, carried on waves of competition and greed.

Sometimes mysteries arrive with the spring thaw.

The End
... of the fifth book in the series

# Jim and Ginger's Next Case

Jim and Ginger return in *"The Body in the Bar"* where they take on the case of a boat racing champion found dead in the Salty Breeze bar.

https://mybook.to/TheBodyInTheBar

# Bonus Content

Get a FREE Jim and Ginger story!

Enjoy "The Curious Case of the Creeping Hedge" – an exclusive short story not available anywhere else!

Subscribe to Arthur Pearce's newsletter today and receive:

- Your free short story
- Updates on new releases
- Special discounts and cover reveals

https://www.arthurpearce.com/newsletter

# Jim and Ginger's First Case

New to the series? Start with *"Murder Next Door"* where Jim and Ginger take on their first case when a friendly neighbor turns up dead.

https://mybook.to/MurderNextDoor

Printed in Dunstable, United Kingdom